**Larenz let out a sigh. Yet even as his body tingled and remembered and longed for more, his mind was listing reasons to walk away from Ellery Dunant right now.**

Tonight had been a mistake. He chose his bed partners carefully, made sure they knew exactly what to expect from him: nothing. Yet Ellery had given herself—her innocence—to him. Larenz turned away from the window, unable to deal with the scalding sense of shame that poured through him. He didn't bed virgins. He didn't break their hearts.

Larenz had no intention of sticking around for Ellery Dunant to fall in love with him. Larenz knew that happy endings like the one Ellery was undoubtedly envisaging didn't exist. He knew it from the hard reality of his own life, his own disappointments…and he had no intention of experiencing that kind of rejection again.

Yet even as he made those resolutions Larenz couldn't quite keep his mind from picturing Ellery's violet eyes, his body from remembering how soft and silken she'd felt in his arms. And he couldn't keep both his mind and body from wanting more.

**Kate Hewitt** discovered her first Mills & Boon® romance on a trip to England when she was thirteen, and she's continued to read them ever since. She wrote her first story at the age of five, simply because her older brother had written one and she thought she could do it too. That story was one sentence long—fortunately they've become a bit more detailed as she's grown older. She has written plays, short stories, and magazine serials for many years, but writing romance remains her first love. Besides writing, she enjoys reading, travelling, and learning to knit.

After marrying the man of her dreams—her older brother's childhood friend—she lived in England for six years, and now resides in Connecticut with her husband, her three young children, and the possibility of one day getting a dog. Kate loves to hear from readers—you can contact her through her website: www.kate-hewitt.com

*A7-*

# THE UNDOING
# OF DE LUCA

BY
KATE HEWITT

MILLS & BOON

First published in Great Britain 2010
Harlequin Mills & Boon Limited,
Eton House, 18-24 Paradise Road, Richmond, Surrey TW9 1SR

© Kate Hewitt 2010

ISBN: 978 0 263 21410 9

Harle  ...ills & Boon policy is to use papers that are  ...al,
rene  ...ble and rec...  ...om  ...  ...vn in
susta  ...able  ...ing and manufacturing  ...  onform
to the  ...  ...  ...n.

Print  ...and  ...nd
by C  ...owe, Chippenham, Wiltshire

# THE UNDOING
# OF DE LUCA

# CHAPTER ONE

HER eyes, he decided, were the most amazing shade of lavender. The colour of a bruise.

'Larenz, did you hear a word I was saying?'

Reluctantly, Larenz de Luca pulled his fascinated gaze from the face of the waitress and turned back to his dining partner. Despite his growing interest in the lovely young woman who had served him his soup, he couldn't fathom why his head of PR had brought him to this manor house. The place was a wreck.

Amelie Weyton drummed her glossy French-manicured nails on the polished surface of the antique dining table, which looked as if it could serve at least twenty, although there were only the two of them seated there now. 'Really, I think this place is perfect.'

Amused, Larenz let his gaze slide back to the waitress. 'Yes,' he murmured, 'I quite agree.' He glanced down at the bowl of soup she had placed in front of him. It was the colour of fresh cream with just a hint of gold and a faint scent of rosemary. He dipped in his spoon. Cream of parsnip. Delicious.

Amelie drummed her fingernails again; Larenz saw a tiny crescent-shaped divot appear on the glossy surface of the table. From the corner of his eye, he saw the waitress flinch but when he looked up her face was carefully expressionless, just as it had been since he'd arrived at Maddock Manor an hour ago. Larenz could tell she didn't like him.

He'd seen it the moment he had crossed the threshold. Lady Maddock's eyes had narrowed and her nostrils had flared even as she'd smiled in welcome. Now her violet gaze swept over him in one quick and quelling glance, and Larenz could tell she was not impressed. The thought amused him.

He was used to assessing people, sizing them up and deciding whether they were useful or not. It was how he'd fought his way up to run his own highly successful business; it was how he stayed on top. And while Lady Maddock may have decided he was an untitled, moneyed nobody, he was beginning to think she was very interesting indeed. And possibly very…useful…as well.

In bed.

'You haven't even seen the grounds yet,' Amelie continued. She took a tiny sip of soup; Larenz knew she wouldn't eat more than a bite or two of the three-course meal Lady Maddock had prepared for them. Ellery Dunant was cook, waitress *and* chatelaine of Maddock Manor. It must gall her terribly to wait on them, Larenz thought with cynical amusement. Or, perhaps, on anyone. Both he and Amelie had acquired plenty of polish but they were still untitled, the dreaded nouveau riche, and, no matter how much money you had, nothing could quite clean the stink of the slum from you. He knew it well.

'The grounds?' he repeated, arching an eyebrow. 'Are they really so spectacular?' He heard the mocking incredulity in his own voice and, from the way he saw Ellery flinch out of the corner of his eye, he knew she had heard it, too.

Amelie gave a sharp little laugh. 'I don't know if *spectacular* is really the word. But it will be perfect—' Her soup forgotten, she'd propped her elbows on the table—Amelie had never quite learned her manners—and now gestured wildly with her hands, knocking her wine glass onto the ancient and rather threadbare Oriental carpet.

Larenz gazed down impassively at the fallen glass—at least it hadn't broken—and the spreading, scarlet stain. He heard Ellery's sharply sucked-in breath and she dropped to her knees in front of him, reaching for the tea towel she'd kept tucked into her waist to blot rather hopelessly at the stain.

He gazed at her bent head, her white-blonde hair scraped up into a sorry little bun. It was an unflattering hairstyle, although at this angle it revealed the pale tender skin at the back of her neck; Larenz had a sudden impulse to press his fingers there and see if her fresh and creamy skin was as soft as it looked. 'I believe a little diluted vinegar gets red wine out of fabric,' he commented politely.

Ellery glanced up swiftly, her eyes narrowing. They were no longer lavender, Larenz observed, but dark violet. The colour of storm clouds, which was rather appropriate as she was obviously furious.

'Thank you,' she said in a voice of arctic politeness. She had the cut-glass tones of the English upper crust; you couldn't fake that accent. God knew, Larenz had once tried, briefly, when he'd been sent to Eton for one hellish year. He'd been scorned and laughed at, easily labelled as a pretender, a poser. He'd walked out before he'd sat his exams— before they could expel him. He'd never gone back to another school of any kind. Life had provided the best education.

Ellery rose from the floor and, as she did so, Larenz caught a faint whiff of her perfume—except it wasn't perfume, he decided, but rather the scent of the kitchen. A kitchen garden, perhaps, for she smelled like wild herbs: rosemary and a faint hint of something else, maybe thyme.

Delicious.

'And, while you're at it,' Amelie drawled in a bored voice, 'perhaps you could bring me another glass of wine?' She arched one perfectly plucked eyebrow, her generous collagen-inflated lips curving in a smile that did not bother to disguise her malice. Larenz suppressed a sigh. Sometimes Amelie could be rather…obvious. He'd known her since his first days starting out in London, sixteen years old and an errand boy at a department store. She'd been working in the shop where Larenz bought sandwiches for the businessmen to eat at their board meetings. She'd cleaned up quite nicely, but she hadn't really changed. Larenz doubted if anyone ever did.

'You don't,' he commented after Ellery had walked swiftly out of the dining room, the green baize-covered door swinging shut behind her, 'have to be quite so rude.'

Amelie shrugged. 'She's been arsey with me since I arrived. Looking down that prim little nose at me. Lady Muck thinks she's better than anyone, but look at this hovel.' She glanced contemptuously around the dining room with its tattered curtains and discoloured patches on the wall where there had surely once been original paintings. 'Her father may have been a baron, but this place is a wreck.'

'And yet you said it was spectacular,' Larenz commented dryly. He took a sip of wine; despite the wreck of a house this manor appeared to be, the wine was a decidedly good vintage. 'Why did you bring me here, Amelie?'

'Spectacular was your word, not mine,' Amelie returned swiftly. 'It's a mouldering wreck, there's no denying it.' She leaned forward. 'That's the point, Larenz. The *contrast*. It will be perfect for the launch of Marina.'

Larenz merely arched an eyebrow. He couldn't quite see how a decrepit manor house was the appropriate place to launch the new line of haute couture that De Luca's, his upmarket department store, had commissioned. But then perhaps this was why Amelie was his head of PR; she had vision.

He simply had determination.

'Imagine it, Larenz, gorgeous gowns in jewel tones—
they'll stand out amazingly against all the musty gloom—a
perfect backdrop, the juxtaposition of old and new, past and
future, where fashion has *been* and where it's going—'

'It all sounds rather artistic,' Larenz murmured. He had no
real interest in the artistry of a photo shoot; he simply wanted
the line to succeed. And, since he was backing it, it would.

'It'll be amazing,' Amelie promised, her Botoxed face
actually showing signs of animation. 'Trust me.'

'I suppose I'll have to,' Larenz replied lightly. 'But did
we have to *sleep* here?'

Amelie laughed lightly. 'Poor Larenz, having to rough it
for a night.' She clucked. 'How will you manage?' Her smile
turned coy. 'Of course, I know a way we could both be more
comfortable—'

'Not a chance, Amelie,' he replied dryly. Every once in
a while, Amelie attempted to get him into bed. Larenz knew
better than to ever mix business and pleasure, and he could
tell Amelie's attempt was half-hearted at best. Amelie was
one of the few people who had known him when he was a
young nobody; it was one of the reasons he allowed her so
much licence. Yet even she knew not to get too close, not to
push too hard. No one—and in particular no woman—was
allowed those kinds of privileges. Ever. A night, a week,
sometimes a little more, was all he allowed his lovers.

Yet, Larenz acknowledged with some amusement,
here was Amelie thinking they might get up to something
amidst all this mould and rot. The thought was appalling,
although...

Larenz's glance slid back to Lady Maddock. She'd returned to the dining room, her lovely face devoid of any
make-up or expression, a glass of wine in one hand and a
litre of vinegar in the other. She carefully placed the glass in
front of Amelie and then, with a murmur of apology, knelt
on the floor again and began to dab at the stain. The stinging

smell of vinegar wafted up towards Larenz, destroying any possible enjoyment of the remainder of his soup.

Amelie hissed in annoyance. 'Can't you do that a bit later?' she asked, making a big show of having to move her legs out of the way while Ellery scrubbed at the stain. 'We're trying to eat.'

Ellery looked up; the vigorous scrubbing had pinkened her cheeks and her eyes now had a definite steely glint.

'I'm sorry, Miss Weyton,' she said evenly, not sounding apologetic at all, 'but if the stain sets in I'll never get it out.'

Amelie made a show of inspecting the worn carpet. 'I hardly think this old thing is worth saving,' she commented dryly. 'It's practically rags already.'

Ellery's flush deepened. 'This carpet,' she returned with icy politeness, 'is a nearly three-hundred-year-old original Aubusson. I have to disagree with you. It's most certainly worth saving.'

'Not like some of the other things in this place, I suppose?' Amelie returned, her gaze moving rather pointedly to the empty patches on the wall, the wallpaper several shades darker there than anywhere else.

If it was possible, Ellery's flush deepened even more. She looked, Larenz thought, magnificent. He'd first thought her a timid little mouse but now he saw she had courage and pride. His lips curved. Not that she had much to be proud about, but she certainly was beautiful.

She rose from her place at their feet in one graceful movement, retrieving the bottle of vinegar and tucking the dirty cloth back into the pocket of her apron.

'Excuse me,' she said stiffly and walked quickly from the room.

'Bitch,' Amelie said, almost idly, and Larenz felt a little flash of disappointment that she had gone.

\* \* \*

Ellery's hands shook as she rinsed out the rag and returned the vinegar to the larder. Rage coursed through her, and she clenched her hands into fists at her sides, pacing the huge kitchen several times as she took in great cleansing breaths in an attempt to calm her fury.

She'd handled that badly; those two were her *guests*. It was so hard to remember that, to accept their snide jibes and careless remarks. They thought paying a few hundred pounds gave them the right, yet Ellery knew it did not. They gave mere money while she gave her life, her very blood, to this place. And she couldn't bear to have it talked about the way that callous crane of a woman had, wrinkling her nose at the carpets and curtains; Ellery knew they were threadbare but that didn't make them any less precious to her.

She'd disliked Amelie Weyton from the moment she'd driven up the Manor's long sweeping drive that afternoon. She'd been at the wheel of a tiny toy of a convertible and had gone too fast so the gravel had sprayed all over the grass and deep ruts had been left in the soft rain-dampened ground. Ellery had said nothing, knowing she couldn't risk losing Amelie as her customer; she'd rented out the manor house for the weekend and the five hundred pounds was desperately needed.

Only that morning the repair man had told her the kitchen boiler was on its very last legs and a new one would cost three thousand pounds.

Ellery had swayed in horror. Three *thousand* pounds? She hadn't earned that kind of money, even with several months at her part-time teaching job in the nearby village. Yet the news should hardly surprise her for, from the moment she'd taken over the running of her ancestral home six months ago, there had been one calamity after another. Maddock Manor was no more than a wreck on its way to near certain ruin.

The best Ellery could do was slow its inevitable decline. Yet she didn't like thinking like this, couldn't think like this, not when holding on to the Manor sometimes felt akin to holding on to herself, the only way she could, even if only for a little while.

Most of the time she was able to push such fears away. She focused on the pressing practical concerns, which were certainly enough to keep both her mind and body occupied.

And so Ellery had kept her focus on that much-needed boiler as Amelie had strolled through the house as if she owned the place.

'This place really is a disaster,' she'd said, dropping her expensive faux-fur coat on one chair; it slithered to the floor and she glanced pointedly at Ellery to pick it up. Biting down hard on the inside of her cheek, Ellery had done so. 'Larenz is going to have a *fit*,' Amelie added, half to herself. Ellery didn't miss the way the woman's mouth caressed the single word: Larenz. An Italian toy boy, she surmised with disgust. 'This is a step—or ten—down for him.' Her eyes glinted with malicious humour as she glanced at Ellery. 'However, I suppose we can rough it for a night or two. It's not like there's anything else around here, is it?'

Ellery forced a polite smile. 'Is your companion arriving soon?' she asked, still holding the wretched woman's coat. When Amelie had emailed the reservation, she'd simply said 'and guest'. Ellery presumed this guest was the aforementioned Larenz.

'Yes, he'll be here for dinner,' Amelie informed her idly. She turned around in a slow circle, taking in the drawing room in all of its shabbiness. 'Good heavens, it's even worse than the photos on the website, isn't it?' she drawled, and Ellery forced herself not to say anything.

She'd chosen photographs of the best rooms for her website, Maddock Holiday Lettings. The conservatory, with throw pillows carefully covering the threadbare patches on the sofa and the sunlight pouring in, bathing the room in mellow gold; the best bedroom, which she'd had redecorated with new linens and curtains.

It had set her back a thousand pounds but she'd been realistic. You couldn't charge people to sleep on tattered sheets.

Still, Amelie's contempt of her home rankled. This venture, letting the Manor out to holidaymakers, was new, and Amelie, in fact, was only the second guest to actually come and stay. The other had been a kindly elderly couple who had been endearingly delighted with everything. They'd appreciated the beauty and history of a house that had stayed in the same family for nearly five hundred years.

Amelie and her Italian lover just saw the stains and the tears.

'And they're making a few more while they're at it,' Ellery muttered under her breath now. She pictured the scarlet splash of red wine on the Aubusson once more and she groaned aloud.

'Are you quite all right?'

Ellery whirled around; she'd been so lost in her thoughts that she hadn't heard the man—Larenz—enter the kitchen. He'd arrived only a few minutes before dinner had been served and Ellery hadn't really had time to greet or even look at him properly. Yet she'd seen enough to form an opinion: Larenz de Luca was not the toy boy she'd expected. He was much worse.

From the moment he'd arrived, Amelie had flirted and fawned over him, yet Larenz had been impervious and even indifferent to the attentions of the gorgeous, if rather emaciated, Amelie, and every careless or callous remark or look had grated on Ellery's nerves, which was ridiculous because she didn't even like Amelie.

Yet she *hated* men who treated women like playthings just to be enjoyed and then discarded. Men like her father.

Ellery forced such negative thoughts away and nodded

stiffly at Larenz. He lounged in the doorway of the kitchen, one shoulder propped against the frame, his deep blue eyes alight with amusement.

He was laughing at her. Ellery had sensed it before, when she'd been scrubbing at the stain. He'd enjoyed seeing her on her knees, working like a skivvy in front of him. She'd seen the smile curl the corner of his mouth—his lips were as perfectly sculpted as a Renaissance statue's—and the same smile was quirking them now as he watched her pace the kitchen.

'I'm perfectly fine, thank you,' she said. 'May I help?'

'Yes, you may, actually,' he returned, his voice a drawl with only a hint of an Italian accent. 'We've finished the soup and we're waiting for the next course.'

'Of course.' She felt colour flare in her face. How long had she been wool-gathering in the kitchen while they waited for their meal? 'I'll be right out.'

Larenz nodded but he didn't move, his eyes lazily sweeping over her, assessing and dismissing all in one bored glance. Ellery could hardly blame him for it; she was dressed in a serviceable black skirt and a white blouse with a sauce stain on the shoulder, and the heat from the kitchen was making her sweaty. Still, his obvious contempt aggravated her, and was so typical of a man like him.

'Good,' he finally said and pushed off from the doorframe, disappearing back into the dining room without another word.

Ellery hurried to check on the chicken simmering on the stove. Fortunately, the tarragon cream sauce hadn't curdled.

Back in the dining room, Amelie and Larenz sat unspeaking. Larenz looked relaxed, sprawled in his seat, while Amelie seemed tense, drumming her nails once more, the little clicks seeming to echo through the silent room. She had, Ellery saw, caused another divot in the ancient tabletop.

Amelie had barely touched her soup but Ellery saw, to her satisfaction, that Larenz had completely cleaned his bowl. As she reached for the empty dish, he laid a hand on her wrist, shocking her with the unexpected touch. His skin was warm and dry and it sent a strange, not unpleasant, jolt right down to her plimsoll-encased toes.

'The soup was delicious,' he murmured, and Ellery jerked her head in the semblance of a nod.

'Thank you. Your main course will be out shortly.' Nerves caused her hands to tremble and the bowl clanked against his wine glass as she took it, making her flush and Larenz smile lazily.

'Careful. You don't want to spill another glass of wine.'

'Your glass is empty,' Ellery returned tartly. She hated that he'd seen how he affected her—and why should he affect her? He was incredibly attractive, yes, but he was also an arrogant ass. 'I'll refill it in a moment,' she added, and turned back to the kitchen.

Dumping the dishes in the sink, Ellery hurried to serve the plates of chicken, sauce and the roasted new potatoes she'd left crisping in the oven. Quite suddenly, she felt utterly exhausted. She had an entire weekend of catering meals—and enduring Amelie's snide remarks and Larenz's speculative looks—ahead of her, yet all she wanted was to go upstairs and hide under the covers.

Behind her, the boiler clanked mournfully and Ellery gritted her teeth. She had to bear it. The only other option was to sell Maddock Manor, and that was no option at all. Not yet, at least. The Manor was the only thing she had left of her family, her father. Sometimes, as impossible and irrational as she knew it was, the Manor felt like the only thing that validated who she was and where she had come from.

She was keeping it.

\* \* \*

Two hours later, Larenz and Amelie had finally retired upstairs. Ellery scraped the remains of their meal—Larenz had finished both his main course and a generous slice of chocolate gâteau, while Amelie had barely touched any of it—into the bin and tried to ease the persistent ache in her lower back. What she really wanted was a long soak in a very hot bath, but the repair man had already told her that such a venture would push the boiler past its limited endurance. She'd have to settle for a hot-water bottle instead, which had been her companion most nights anyway. Now that it was late October, the cold stole into the Manor and crouched in corners, especially in the draughty, unheated room where Ellery slept.

Sighing, she stacked the rinsed plates in the dishwasher and mentally ran through her to-do list for breakfast. Part of the weekend package was a full English fry-up, yet she was quite sure Amelie Weyton ran only to black coffee in the mornings.

Larenz, on the other hand, probably required a hearty breakfast that he'd tuck into with relish while never putting on an ounce. Quite suddenly, Ellery found her mind wandering upstairs, to the best bedroom with its antique four-poster—the new silk hangings had eaten up most of her budget for the room's redecoration—and the birch logs she'd laid in the hearth that morning. Would Larenz light a fire so he and Amelie could be cosy in bed together, the flames casting dancing shadows over the bed and their entangled bodies?

Or perhaps they would have another source of heat—she imagined them there, among the pillows and blankets, Amelie's limbs twined around Larenz, and felt a sudden dart of completely unreasonable jealousy.

She could not possibly be jealous. What was there to be jealous of? She despised the pair of them. Yet even as she asked herself this, Ellery already knew the answer. She was jealous of Amelie having someone—anyone—but especially someone as attractive and, face it, as sexy as Larenz de Luca. She was jealous of them both, and the fact that neither of them would be alone tonight. Like she would.

Ellery sighed. She'd been living at Maddock Manor, attempting to make ends if not meet, at least glimpse each other, for six long, lonely months. She'd made a few friends in the village, but nothing like the life she'd once had. Nothing like the life she wanted.

Her university friends were all in London, living the young urban lifestyle that she'd once, ridiculously, enjoyed. Even after only half a year it seemed as faded and foggy as a dream, the kind where you could only remember hazy fragments and surreal snatches. Her best friend, Lil, was constantly urging her to come back to London, even if just for a visit, and Ellery had managed it once.

Yet one weekend in the city didn't completely combat the loneliness of living alone in an abandoned manor house, day after day after day. Ellery shook her head in an attempt to rid herself of such useless thoughts. She was acting maudlin and pathetic and it annoyed her. She couldn't visit London right now, but she could at least ring her friend. She imagined telling Lil all about the horrible Amelie and Larenz and knew her friend would relish the gossip.

Smiling at the thought, Ellery resumed stacking the dishwasher and wiping the worktops. She had just finished and was about to switch off the lights when a voice made her jump nearly a foot in the air.

'Excuse me—'

Ellery whirled around, one hand to her chest. Larenz de Luca stood in the kitchen doorway, leaning against the door. How had she not heard him come in again? He must, she thought resentfully, be as quiet as a cat. He smiled sleepily, and Ellery noticed how deliciously rumpled he looked. His hair, glinting darkly in the light, curled over his forehead and was just a little ruffled. He'd shed his suit jacket and tie from earlier and had unbuttoned the top two buttons of his shirt; Ellery could glimpse a stretch of golden skin there, at the base of his throat, that made her suddenly swallow rather dryly.

'Did I frighten you?' he asked, and she thought his accent sounded more pronounced. It was probably intentional, Ellery thought with a twinge of cynical amusement. He did the sexy Italian thing rather well, and he knew it.

'You startled me,' she corrected, sounding as crisp and buttoned-up as the spinster schoolteacher she was for the children in the village. She gave him her best teacher's glare and was satisfied to see him inadvertently straighten. 'Is there something you need, Mr de Luca?'

Larenz cocked his head, his heavy-lidded gaze sweeping over her as it had earlier that night. 'Yes, there is,' he finally said, still in that sleepy yet speculative voice. 'I wondered if I could have a glass of water.'

'There are glasses and a pitcher in your room,' Ellery replied, and heard the implied rebuke in her voice. Larenz heard it too, for he arched his eyebrows, his mouth quirking—Ellery couldn't tear her gaze away from those amazing lips—and said, 'Perhaps, but I prefer ice.'

Somehow she managed to drag her gaze upwards, to those blue, blue eyes that were so clearly laughing at her. She managed a stiff nod. 'Of course. Just a moment.'

She felt Larenz's eyes on her as she went to the chest freezer and rifled through the economy-sized bags of peas and chicken cutlets.

'Do you live here alone?' he asked, his tone now one of scrupulous politeness.

Ellery finally located a bag of ice and pulled it out, slamming the lid of the freezer down with a bit more force than necessary. 'Yes.'

She saw his glance move around the huge empty kitchen. 'You don't have any help?'

Surely that was obvious, considering how she'd cooked and waited on them tonight. 'A boy from the village mows the lawns every now and then.' She didn't want to admit just how alone she really was, how sometimes the house seemed to stretch in endless emptiness all around her so she felt as tiny and insignificant as one of the many dust motes filtering through the stale air. She *really* needed to ring Lil and get some perspective.

Larenz raised his brows again and Ellery knew what he was thinking. The lawns were bedraggled and rather over-grown; she hadn't had the money to pay Darren to mow recently. So what? she wanted to demand. It was nearly winter anyway. No one mowed their lawns in winter, did they?

She dumped the ice into two glasses and thrust them at Larenz, her chin lifted. 'Will that be all?'

His mouth quirked again as he glanced at the glasses—Ellery realized she'd assumed Amelie wanted ice too—and then he took the glasses, his fingers sliding across hers. The simple touch of skin on skin made Ellery jerk back as if she'd been scalded. She felt as if she had; she could still feel the warmth of his hand even though he was no longer touching her.

She hated that she reacted so obviously to his little touches—his intentional little touches, for there could be no doubting that he did it on purpose, just to see her jump. To enjoy how he affected her, for wasn't that the basic source of power of a man over a woman? And here she was, hating Larenz de Luca yet still in his thrall. The thought made Ellery's face flame with humiliated aggravation.

Larenz's mouth curled into a fully fledged smile, lighting his eyes, turning them to a gleaming sapphire. 'Goodnight, Lady Maddock.'

Ellery stiffened. She didn't use her title—worthless as it was—and it sounded faintly mocking on Larenz's lips. Her father had been a baron and the title had died out with him. Her own was no more than a courtesy, an affectation.

Still, she had no desire to continue the conversation so she merely jerked her head in acceptance and, with another sleepy smile, Larenz turned around and left.

Suddenly, in spite of her best intentions to have him walk away without another word, Ellery heard herself calling out, 'What time do you eat breakfast?'

Larenz paused, glancing at her over his shoulder. 'I usually like to eat early, although, since it is the weekend…would nine o'clock be all right?' His lips twitched. 'I'd like to give you a bit of a lie-in.'

Ellery glared at him. The man could make anything sound suggestive and even sensual, and she certainly didn't need his consideration. 'Thank you, but that's really not necessary. I'm an early riser.'

'Then perhaps we'll watch the dawn together,' Larenz murmured and, with a last wicked smile that let her know he knew just how much he was teasing—and even affecting—her, he left, the door swinging shut behind him with a breathy sigh.

Ellery counted to ten, and then on to twenty, and then she swore aloud. She waited until she heard Larenz's footsteps on the stairs—the third one always creaked—and then she reached for the telephone. It was late, but Lil was almost always ready for a chat.

She picked up on the second ring. 'Ellery? Tell me you've finally come to your senses.'

Ellery gave a little laugh as she brought the telephone into the larder, where there was less chance of being overheard in case Larenz or Amelie ventured downstairs again.

'Just about, after tonight,' she said and Lil laughed, the pulsing beat of club music audible from her end.

'Thank heavens. I don't know why you shut yourself away up there—'

Ellery closed her eyes, a sudden shaft of pain, unexpected and sharp, slicing through her. 'You know why, Lil.'

Lil sighed. They'd had this conversation too many times already. No matter how many times Ellery tried to explain it, her friend couldn't understand why she'd thrown away a busy, full life in London for taking care of a mouldering manor. Ellery didn't blame Lil for not understanding; she barely understood it herself. Returning to Maddock Manor when her mother had been preparing to sell it had been a gut decision. Emotional and irrational. She accepted that, yet it didn't change how she felt, or how much she needed to stay. For now, at least.

'So what happened tonight?' Lil asked.

'Oh, I have these awful guests,' Ellery said lightly. Suddenly she didn't feel like regaling Lil with stories of Amelie and Larenz. 'Completely OTT and high maintenance.'

'Throw the tossers out, then,' Lil said robustly. 'Take a train—'

'Lil, I can't. I have to stay here until—' Ellery stopped, not wanting to finish the thought.

'Until the money runs out?' Lil filled in for her. 'When will that be? Another two weeks?'

Ellery managed a wobbly laugh. 'More like three.' She sighed, sliding to the floor, her forehead resting on her knees. 'I know I'm mad.'

'At least you admit it,' Lil replied cheerfully. 'Look, I know you can't come now, but you are due for a visit. That manor is bringing you down, Ellery, and you need someone to bring you *up*.' Her voice softened. 'Come back to the city, have fun, have a real relationship for starters—'

'Don't,' Ellery warned with a sigh, even though she knew her friend was right.

'Why not? It's not like you're going to meet a man in the bowels of Suffolk, and you don't want to die a virgin, do you?'

Ellery winced. Lil was her best friend, but sometimes she was just a bit too blunt. And she'd never really understood how—or why—Ellery had kept herself from the messy complications of sex and love for so long. 'I'm not looking for some kind of fling,' she said, even as an image—a tempting image—of Larenz flitted through her mind, his tie loosened and his hair tousled...

'Well, how about a girls' weekend, then?' Lil suggested.

'Now *that* sounds lovely—'

'But?' Lil interjected knowingly. 'What's your excuse this time, Ellery?'

'No excuses,' Ellery replied a bit more firmly than she felt. 'I know I need to get away, Lil. I nearly lost my temper with these idiot guests and it's just because I haven't been anywhere or done anything but try to keep things together here—'

'Then next weekend,' Lil cut her off kindly, for Ellery knew she sounded too emotional. Felt too emotional. She didn't like showing so much of herself, being so vulnerable, not even with Lil, and her friend knew it. 'You don't have any guests booked then?'

'Not hardly.' She injected a cheerful note into her voice. 'This lot's only my second. Thanks for chatting, Lil, but I can tell you're out on the town—'

A peal of raucous laughter sounded from Lil's end. 'It doesn't matter—'

'And I'm exhausted,' Ellery finished. 'I'll talk to you later.' After she'd disconnected the call, Ellery sat there, the receiver pressed to her chest, the manor house quiet and dark all around her. She could hear the wind blowing outside, a lost, lonely sound.

The phone call had made her feel a bit better, and she was *definitely* going to go to London next weekend, but in the meantime this weekend—with its two guests—still yawned endlessly in front of her. Sighing, Ellery rose and replaced the telephone before heading to bed.

Upstairs, Larenz took his two glasses, the ice cubes clinking against each other, and walked past Amelie's door. She'd taken the best bed for herself—of course—and Larenz knew the only way to enjoy such comfort was to share it. When they'd gone upstairs together, Amelie still chattering on about how perfect this wreck of a house would be for the launch of Marina, Larenz had known with a certain weariness that the moment was coming.

And so it had, with Amelie pausing in the doorway of the best bedroom, giving him a kittenish little smile that might have amused him once, but now just annoyed him.

'It's awfully cold in here, you know,' she said in a husky murmur.

'You could ask Lady Maddock for a hot-water bottle,' he replied dryly, stepping back from Amelie's open doorway just so she got the message.

She did, smiling easily. That was one good thing about Amelie; she caught on quickly. 'I'm sure she's using it for herself,' she replied. 'It's probably the only thing that ever shares her bed,' she added with that touch of malice Larenz had never really liked.

'Well, at least you have lots of covers,' he replied lightly. From her open doorway, he caught a glimpse of an ornate four-poster piled high with throw pillows and a satin duvet. It looked a good deal more comfortable than the spartan room he'd had to settle for.

Still, he wasn't even tempted. Especially not when his mind—and other parts of his body—still recalled the way Ellery Dunant's violet eyes had flashed at him, the way she'd jerked in response to his lightest touch. She wanted him. She didn't want to want him, but she did.

He turned back to Amelie, the friendliness in his voice

now replaced with flat finality. 'Goodnight, Amelie.' He turned away and walked to his own bedroom without looking back.

Back in his own room now, Larenz grimaced at the faded wallpaper and worn coverlet. Clearly, Lady Maddock had not got around to redecorating the other bedrooms.

He put aside his glass with the precious ice—it had been no more than a pretext to see Ellery Dunant again—and pulled the covers down from the bed. A gust of wind rattled the windowpanes and Larenz felt the icy draught. He grimaced again. What on earth was Ellery Dunant doing in a place like this? Clearly her family had fallen on hard times, but Larenz couldn't fathom why she didn't sell up and move somewhere more congenial. She was young, pretty and obviously talented to some degree. Why was she wasting away in the far reaches of Suffolk taking care of a house that looked about to collapse around her ears?

Shrugging the thought aside, Larenz began to undress. He normally slept in just his boxers but it was so damned cold in this place he decided to leave his shirt and socks on, making him look, he suspected, rather ridiculous.

He doubted Ellery Dunant's room was properly heated. He pictured her in a white cotton nightdress, the kind that buttoned right up to her neck, a pair of fuzzy slippers on her feet, clutching a hot-water bottle. The image made his lips twitch in amusement until he found his mind leaping ahead to the moment when he unbuttoned that starchy nightgown and discovered the delectable woman underneath.

She'd been affected by him; there could be no denying that. Larenz recalled the way her skin had felt, as soft as silk and faintly cool. Her fingernails, he'd noticed, had been bitten to the quick. She was undoubtedly worried about finances; why else would she be renting out this decrepit place?

He knew just how to take her mind off such matters.

He stretched out in bed, wincing at the icy sheets. Again,

he found himself imagining Ellery there with him, warming the sheets, warming him.

And he could warm her... He would take great pleasure in thawing the ice princess, Larenz thought, folding his hands behind his head. Sleep seemed a long way off. From outside he heard a telltale creak of the floorboards and hoped it wasn't Amelie making a last-ditch effort. Surely she had more pride than that; their working relationship was too important to throw away on an ill-conceived fling.

His mind roved back to Ellery. He wondered whether she was pining away for some prince while she waited in her lonely manor. Was she hoping for some would-be knight to rescue her? Well, he was no knight or prince, not in the least. He was a bastard through and through and there was surely no way Lady Maddock would consider him as husband material for a second, which suited him fine.

But as a lover...? Larenz smiled and settled more deeply into the bed.

Then he heard the floorboard creak again, past his room, and the sound of a door closing somewhere at the other end of the hall. It must have been Ellery, on her way to bed.

Larenz stretched out, trying to make himself more comfortable despite the rather lumpy mattress and the coldness of the room. Had Ellery walked past his room on purpose? Was she curious? Longing?

He hoped so, because he had just decided that she most definitely needed to be seduced.

# CHAPTER TWO

ELLERY woke early, determined to fill the day with chores and errands. If she kept herself busy and productive, she'd have less time to think. Imagine.

It had been imagining that had kept her up last night, restless with a nameless longing that had suddenly risen up inside her, a tide of need. She'd replayed the moments with Larenz, the feel of his fingers on her skin, over and over again, hating herself for doing so. Hating him.

She needed to focus, she told herself as she tied an apron around her waist and reached for a dozen eggs from inside the fridge. Focus on getting work done now and then having a weekend away, as she'd promised Lil. She tried to imagine herself in London at some random club or bar, having *fun*, but the image remained both blurry and vaguely depressing.

'It *would* be fun,' Ellery insisted in a mutter as she cracked six eggs into a heavy china mixing bowl and began to whip them into a foamy froth. 'We'd talk and laugh and dance—' And Lil would try to convince her—again—to come back to London.

When Ellery had told her friend she was returning home in an attempt to make Maddock Manor a success, Lil had looked at her as if she'd gone completely mad.

'Why on earth would you want to go back *there*?'

Ellery hadn't been able to answer that question. She'd only

visited her home once or twice a year since her father had died; her mother usually preferred to meet her in London. She had never even had much affection for the house, really; four years at boarding school and another three at university had made her a stranger to the place, and she still remembered the shock slicing through her at its decrepit state when she'd returned after her mother had announced she planned to sell it. When had the paintings been sold? When had the grounds gone to ruin? Had she never noticed, or had she simply not cared? Or, most frighteningly, had their family's slide into financial ruin happened a long time ago, her father hiding the truth from her, as he had with so many things?

Yet, despite the Manor's decrepit state, Ellery had been determined to keep it for as long as she could. Somehow the prospect of losing it—losing her childhood memories there—had forced some latent instinct to kick in and so she'd rushed into this unholy mess. Even now she couldn't regret it, couldn't shake the fear that if she lost the Manor, she lost her father. It was a stupid fear, absurd, because she'd lost her father long, long ago...if she'd ever really had him.

Grimacing, Ellery reached for a tomato from the windowsill and began to slice it with a bit too much vigour. She didn't like to dwell on memories; if she thought too much about the past she started wondering if anything was true... or trustworthy.

'Careful with that. You're liable to lose a finger.' Once again, Ellery jumped and whirled around, the chopping knife still brandished in one hand. Larenz stood in the doorway, looking even better than he had last night. Even in her pique, Ellery could not quite keep herself from gazing at him. He was dressed in a pair of faded jeans and a worn grey T-shirt. Simple clothes, Saturday slumming clothes, Ellery supposed, yet Larenz de Luca looked far too good in them, the soft cotton and faded denim lovingly hugging his powerful frame, emphasizing his trim hips and muscular thighs.

'I'm fine, thank you,' she said crisply. 'And, if you don't mind, I'd rather you knocked before coming into the kitchen.'

'Sorry,' Larenz murmured, sounding utterly unrepentant.

Ellery made herself smile and raised her chin a notch. 'May I help you with something, Mr de Luca? Breakfast should be ready in a few minutes.' She glanced pointedly at the old clock hanging above the stove. It was a quarter to nine.

'Why don't you call me Larenz?' he suggested with a smile.

Ellery's smile back was rather brittle. 'I'm afraid it's not the Manor's policy to address guests by their first names.' That was a complete fabrication and, from Larenz's little smile, she could tell he knew it. He was amused by it.

'The Manor?' he queried softly. 'Or Lady Maddock's?'

'I don't actually use the title,' Ellery said stiffly. She hated her title, hated its uselessness, its deceit. As if she was the only one who deserved it. 'You may simply call me Miss Dunant.' Listening to her crisp voice, she knew she sounded starchy and even absurd. She wished, for a fierce unguarded moment, that she could be someone else. Sound like someone else, light, amused, mocking even. She wished she could feel that way, as if things didn't matter. As if they didn't hurt. Instead, she just bristled and it made Larenz de Luca laugh at her.

'Miss Dunant,' Larenz repeated thoughtfully. 'I'm afraid I usually prefer to be a bit more informal. But if you insist...' He took a step closer, still giving her that lovely lazy smile, and Ellery's heart began to beat like a frightened rabbit's. She sucked in a quick, sharp breath.

'Will Miss Weyton be joining you for breakfast?'

'No, she won't.' Larenz's smile widened. 'As a matter of fact, Miss Weyton is leaving this morning.'

'What…?' Ellery couldn't keep the appalled shock from her voice. She realized she was disappointed, not simply to lose the money, but to lose the company. Larenz de Luca, the most intriguing and infuriating man she'd come across in a long time. She was actually disappointed that he might be leaving.

'Yes, she has to return to work,' Larenz continued, sounding anything but regretful. 'However, I'll be staying for the rest of the weekend.'

Ellery's breath came out in a slow hiss. 'You'll be staying?' she repeated, and heard how ridiculously breathy her voice sounded. Inwardly, she cringed. 'Alone?'

Larenz had been moving slowly towards her so now he was less than a foot away. Ellery could smell the clean citrusy tang of his aftershave, and she found her fascinated gaze resting on the steady pulse in his throat. The skin there looked so smooth and golden.

'Well, I won't be alone,' Larenz murmured. He reached out to tuck an errant tendril of hair behind her ear and Ellery jerked back in shock; her skin seemed to buzz and burn where his fingers had skimmed it. Her senses were too scattered to make a reply and, seeing this, Larenz clarified, 'I'll be with you.'

She took a step backwards, away from both danger and temptation. She didn't want to be tempted, not by a man she couldn't even like. Not by a man who looked poised to use her and discard her—and any other woman—just as her father had her mother.

Or perhaps Larenz de Luca wouldn't even get that far. Perhaps he was simply amusing himself with her, enjoying her obvious and inexperienced reactions. Perhaps he never intended to act on any of this. She didn't know which was more humiliating. 'I'm afraid I'll be busy with my duties most of the weekend,' she told him crisply, 'but I'm sure you'll enjoy the relaxing solitude of Maddock Manor…especially such a busy man as yourself.'

Larenz watched her stumbling retreat with a faint, mocking little smile. 'Am I so busy?' he murmured and Ellery shrugged, spreading her hands wide, forgetting she was still holding a rather wicked-looking knife.

'I'm sure—'

'Watch that,' Larenz murmured, his voice still lazy despite the fact that the knife's blade had swept scant inches from his abdomen.

'Oh—' Ellery returned the knife to the worktop with an inelegant clatter. Her breath came out in an agitated shudder. She hated that this man affected her so much, and she hated it even more that he knew it. 'It's probably better,' she managed, turning back to her bowl of eggs so she didn't have to face him, 'if you leave me to finish making breakfast.'

'As you wish,' Larenz replied. 'But I'm going to hold you to showing me the grounds later today.' He left before Ellery could make a response, but she already knew she had no intention of showing Larenz de Luca anything while he was here. She intended to stay completely out of his way.

The weekend seemed as if it were getting longer by the minute.

Larenz wandered through the empty reception rooms as he waited for Ellery to make his breakfast. The heavy velvet curtains were still drawn against the light, although pale autumn sunshine filtered through the cracks and highlighted the dust motes dancing in the air.

Larenz gazed around the drawing room, with its high ceiling and intricate cornices, a beautiful marble fireplace and long sash windows. It was a stately, elegant room, and if he tried he could almost see it as it had once been, grand and imposing, despite the faded carpets and moth-eaten upholstery, the peeling gilt and wide crack in the marble surround of the fireplace.

He thought he could hear Amelie upstairs rather forcefully throwing her things back into her suitcase. She had been less than pleased to be summarily dismissed from the manor.

Larenz had caught her coming out of her bedroom—she looked as if she'd had a better night's sleep than he had—and said with a little smile, 'I've been thinking about your idea of using the manor as the location for Marina's fashion shoot. It's a good one.'

Amelie's lipsticked mouth curved into a satisfied smile. 'I knew you would.'

'And,' Larenz added in an implacable tone, 'I need you to head back to the office this morning to start the paperwork. I'll deal with Ellery.'

'Ellery, is it?' Amelie noted, her eyes narrowing. She forced a smile. 'Well, I for one will be glad to see the last of this hovel for a little while at least.' Larenz felt only relief as he headed downstairs.

Now, wandering restlessly through the drawing room, Larenz thought of how Ellery had whirled around when he'd come into the kitchen that morning, surprised and jumpy and aware, and he smiled, all thoughts of Amelie wiped clean away. This weekend was going to be very interesting and, he had no doubt, very pleasurable, as well.

Ellery placed the scrambled eggs, fried mushrooms, bacon, stewed tomato and a heap of baked beans on a plate, grabbed the rack of toast and a bottle of ketchup with her free hand, and made her way into the dining room.

Somewhere in the distance a door slammed and Ellery winced at the sound of a car starting, along with the telltale spray of gravel. More ruts in the road.

'That would be Amelie leaving,' Larenz said pleasantly. He stepped from the shadows of the dining room where he'd been standing. Hiding, more like, Ellery thought. At least this time she didn't jump.

'In a hurry, is she?' she asked dryly. She ignored the sudden pounding of her heart and the fact that her mind—and body—were very aware that she and Larenz de Luca were now alone. She placed the food on the table and turned around to fetch the coffee. 'I'll be right back.'

'You are getting a plate for yourself, I hope?' Larenz enquired. A frisson of feeling—could it possibly be hope—shivered through Ellery. She stiffened, her back to him. 'I prefer not to eat alone,' Larenz clarified, a hint of laughter in his voice.

'I eat in the kitchen,' she said without turning around.

'Then allow me to join you.'

She heard Larenz reach for his plate, the clank of cutlery as he scooped up his dishes, quite prepared to follow her into the kitchen. Slowly Ellery turned around. 'What exactly do you want from me, Mr de Luca?'

'Is friendliness not part of the weekend special?' he asked lightly. He didn't answer her question.

'I like to be friendly *and* professional,' she replied curtly.

'As a matter of fact, this is professional,' Larenz returned. 'I have a business proposition to put to you.'

Ellery didn't bother hiding her disbelief. The idea of this wealthy man having anything to do with her or Maddock Manor was utterly absurd. 'You can't be serious—'

Larenz gave her a playful, mocking smile. 'Is that your reaction to most business propositions?'

She gritted her teeth. She'd been doing that quite a bit since Larenz de Luca and his lover had arrived—although now she was gone, no doubt dismissed by Larenz. He'd discarded one woman—and why? To move on to another?

To move on to her?

Ellery pushed the alarming—and tempting—possibility

away. Surely there had to be another reason for his continued presence. He was far too wealthy to enjoy staying in a
place like Maddock Manor; he was clearly used to five-star
hotels with matching service. Amelie had told her as much
yesterday, and everything Ellery had noticed about Larenz de
Luca confirmed this opinion, from the navy-blue Lexus he'd
driven up in last night to the way he stood there, arrogantly
relaxed in his supposed Saturday slumming clothes. He was,
Ellery noticed, wearing buttery-soft loafers of Italian leather
that had to have cost several hundred pounds at least. The
man reeked of power and privilege.

Maddock Manor was way, way beneath him. *She* was
way, way beneath him. And yet he stayed?

It made her nervous, anxious and even a little bit afraid.

'You're clearly a very wealthy, important person,'
she finally said with frank honesty. 'I can't imagine any
business proposition of yours that would involve me or
Maddock—'

'Then you're wrong,' Larenz said softly. 'And my breakfast is getting cold.' He lifted the plate once more. 'Shall
we?'

Ellery capitulated. She realized she had little choice, for
Larenz was clearly the kind of man who was used to getting his own way. And she was tired of fighting; she was
exhausted already. After breakfast she'd fob him off with
the list of errands she had to do. She couldn't quite see him
tagging along while she dug for the last potatoes or raked
over the gravel that Amelie had sprayed everywhere.

'Fine,' she said curtly and then, because it was obvious he
had no intention of being an ordinary guest, she threw over
her shoulder, 'we can eat in the kitchen.'

Ellery fixed herself a plate of eggs and mushrooms while
Larenz took a seat at the big scrubbed pine table. He popped
a mushroom into his mouth and surveyed the huge room with

its original fireplace big enough to roast an ox and the bank of windows letting in the pale morning sunshine.

'I'd say this was quite cosy,' he murmured, 'except this table could seat a round dozen. And I imagine it once did, in this house's heyday.' He smiled, raising his eyebrows. 'When was that?'

Ellery stiffened. 'The house's heyday?' she repeated and then, to her surprise and dismay, she sighed, the sound all too wistful and revealing. 'Probably some time in the seventeenth century. I think the Dunants were originally Puritans in good standing with Cromwell.'

'And did they lose it all in the Restoration?'

Ellery shrugged. 'I don't think so. They changed sides a dozen times or more.' She reached for two heavy china mugs and poured coffee. 'The Dunants aren't particularly known for being faithful.' Too late she heard the spite and bitterness in her voice and closed her eyes, hoping Larenz hadn't heard it, too. Yet, even without turning around, she knew he had; he was far too perceptive for his own good—or hers.

'Here.' She placed a mug of coffee in front of him on the table and then walked around to her own seat, all the way on the other end of the table. It looked a little ridiculous for them to be sitting so far apart but Ellery didn't care. She wasn't about to give Larenz any excuse to touch her.

*Even if you want him to...*

Ellery just barely kept from closing her eyes again. It was a good thing Larenz de Luca wasn't capable of mind reading—except when she looked at him and saw that faint knowing smile on his face she felt as if he was.

'Thank you,' he murmured and took a sip of coffee. Ellery began to eat her eggs with grim determination. She didn't want to talk to Larenz, didn't want him to flirt or tease or tempt her. Yet, even as these thoughts flitted through her mind and her eggs turned rubbery and tasteless in her mouth, Ellery knew she was already tempted. Badly. She thought of how Larenz's flutter of fingers on her wrist, skin sliding on skin, had jolted her, an electric current wired directly to her soul.

Except, Ellery thought as she speared a mushroom, souls had nothing to do with it; the temptation she felt for Larenz de Luca was purely, utterly physical. It had to be, for he was exactly the kind of man she despised. The kind of man her father had been.

She glanced up from her breakfast to look at Larenz, to drink him in, for he really was the most amazingly beautiful man. Her gaze lingered on the straight line of his nose, the slashes of his dark brows, those full moulded lips—she imagined those lips touching her, even somewhere seemingly innocuous, like where his fingers had been, on her wrist—and she nearly shuddered aloud.

'Is something wrong?' Larenz asked. He lifted his mug to take a sip of coffee and his eyes danced over its rim.

'What do you mean?' Ellery asked sharply. She returned her fork to her plate with a clatter. She'd been caught staring, of course, and she pulled her lip between her teeth, nipping hard, at the realization.

Larenz lowered his mug. His eyes still danced. 'It's just you looked a bit—pained.'

'Pained?' Ellery repeated. She rose abruptly from the table and grabbed her plate, moving to scrape the remains of her mostly uneaten breakfast into the bin. 'I'm afraid I have rather a lot on my mind,' she explained tartly. Too much on her mind to be thinking about Larenz the way she had. Too many worries to add temptation to the mix, especially when she knew he could only be amusing himself with her. The thought stung.

'Breakfast was delicious, thank you,' Larenz said. He'd moved to the sink, where Ellery watched in surprise as he rinsed his plate and mug and placed them in the dishwasher.

'Thank you,' she half mumbled, touched by his little thoughtfulness. 'You don't have to clean up—'

'Amazingly, I am capable of putting a few dishes away,' Larenz said with a wry smile that reached right into Ellery and twisted her heart. Or maybe something else. She turned away again, busying herself with the mindless tasks of wiping the table down and turning off the coffeemaker. From the corner of her eye, she saw Larenz lean one shoulder against the door, his hands in the pockets of his jeans. 'So it looks to be a beautiful day out. How about you show me the grounds and we can discuss this business proposition?'

Ellery jerked around, the dripping dishcloth still in her hand. She'd completely forgotten about his business proposition—what kind of proposal could he possibly have?

'I'm really rather busy—' she began and Larenz just smiled.

'I promise you, it'll be worth your while.' He reached out almost lazily and took the dishcloth from her hand, tossing it easily into the sink where it landed with a wet thud. 'An hour of your time, no more. Surely you can spare that?'

Ellery hesitated. Larenz stood there, relaxed and waiting, a faint smile curving those amazing lips, and suddenly she had no more excuses. She didn't even *want* to have any more excuses. She wanted, for once, an hour to enjoy herself. To enjoy temptation instead of resist it. To see what might happen, even if it was dangerous. An hour couldn't hurt, surely? That was all she'd give Larenz—or herself.

She let her breath out slowly. 'All right. But we ought to wear wellies.' She glanced pointedly at his leather loafers. 'It rained last night and it's quite muddy out.'

'I'm afraid,' Larenz murmured, 'I didn't bring any— wellies—with me.'

Ellery pursed her lips. She could just imagine the kind of clothes in the case Larenz had brought inside last night, and it didn't run to rubber boots. 'It's a good job that we have plenty for guests,' she returned, and Larenz quirked one eyebrow in question.

'We?'

'I mean I,' Ellery clarified, flushing. 'The boots are from when I was growing up—when we had house guests.' Her throat suddenly felt tight. She tried not to think of those days, when she was little and Maddock Manor had been full of people and laughter, the rooms gleaming and smelling of fresh flowers and beeswax polish and everything had been happy.

Had seemed happy, she mentally corrected, and went to the utility room to fetch a pair of boots she thought might be in Larenz's size.

Larenz followed Ellery out of the kitchen door to the walled garden adjacent to the Manor. He took in the remnants of a summer garden, now bedraggled and mostly dead, the grass no more than muddy patches. He wondered if the parsnips for last night's soup had come from here. He imagined Ellery harvesting the garden by herself, a lonely, laborious task, and something unexpected pulled at his heart.

He felt a single stab of pity, which was most unlike him. He'd worked too hard for too long pulling himself up from the gutter to feel sorry for an aristocrat who'd fallen on hard times, no doubt in part due to her family's extravagant living.

Yet, as he watched Ellery stride ahead of him, the boots enveloping her slender legs, her back stiff and straight, he realized he did feel a surprising twist of compassion for her.

She would be horrified if she knew. Ellery Dunant, Larenz thought with amusement, possessed a rather touching amount of pride. She seemed to love this heap of hers about as much as she disliked him, and was, he knew, most reluctant to spend time with him. She resented the attraction she felt for him, that much was obvious, but Larenz did not think she could resist its tug for long.

He certainly had no desire to. He wanted to release that platinum fall of hair from its sorry scraped little bun; he wanted to trail his fingers along her creamy skin and see if it was as soft as it looked—everywhere. He wanted to transform the disdain that pinched her face to a desire that would soften it. And he would. He always got what he wanted.

'Did you plant a garden this summer?' Larenz asked, nudging a row of withered runner beans. Ellery turned around, her hands deep in the pockets of her waxed jacket.

'Yes—a small one.' She glanced around the garden, remembering the vision she'd once had, the rows of hollyhocks, the cornucopia of vegetables, the neat little herb garden. She'd managed only a few potatoes and parsnips, things that were easy to grow, for she'd learned rather quickly that she did not have much of a green thumb. 'It's difficult to manage on my own,' she explained stiffly. 'But one day—' She stopped, letting the thought fall to the ground, unnourished. One day what? Every day she stayed at Maddock Manor, Ellery was conscious of how futile her plans really were. She would never get ahead on her own, never have enough money to make the necessary repairs, much less the renovations, never be able to see Maddock Manor restored to the glory it had once known. She tried to avoid these damning realizations, and for the most part she did, simply living day by day. It was Larenz de Luca, with his knowing smile and pointed questions, who reminded her of the futility of her life here.

She turned away from the garden to lead Larenz out to the half-timbered barns that flanked the rear of the property. 'So just what is this business proposition?' she called over her shoulder.

'Let me see the barns,' Larenz returned equably, and Ellery suppressed a groan. She'd only agreed to show Larenz the grounds because she'd already discovered how persistent he could be, and in a moment of folly—weakness—she'd wanted to spend time with him. She'd wanted to feel that dangerous, desirable jolt again. Even—especially—if it went nowhere; there was nowhere for it to go.

Yet, now that they were actually outside, Larenz inspecting the overgrown gardens and crumbling brick walls, Ellery felt no enjoyment or excitement, only the ragged edge of desperation as a man who looked as if he'd never known a day of want or need strolled through the remnants of her own failure.

'A lovely building,' Larenz murmured as Ellery let him into the dim, dusty interior of the barn that had once stabled a dozen workhorses. She blinked in the gloom, the sunlight filtering through the cracks.

'Once,' she agreed, and Larenz just smiled.

'Yours is hardly the first stately home to fall into disrepair.'

Ellery nodded rather glumly. It was a story being told all over England: estates crippled by rising costs and inheritance taxes, turned over to the National Trust or private enterprises, hotels or amusement parks or even, in the case of a manor nearby, a zoo.

Larenz stepped deeper into the dimness of the barn and ran his hand over a bulky shape shrouded in canvas tarpaulin that took over most of the interior. 'Have you ever thought of turning the place into a park or museum?'

'No.' She'd resisted letting Maddock Manor become anything but the home it once had been—her home, her mother's home, a place that had defined them—because she was afraid if she lost the Manor she'd have nothing left. Nothing that pointed to who she was—what she was. Her father's daughter. 'Letting rooms out for holidays is the first step, I suppose, but I couldn't bear it if someone put a roller coaster up in the garden or something like that.'

Larenz turned to her, his eyes glinting with amusement even in the musty dimness of the barn. 'Surely you wouldn't have to do something so drastic.'

Ellery shrugged. 'I don't have the money to renovate it myself, not on a large scale, so the only choice would be to turn it over to developers.'

'Have you had any offers?'

That was the galling bit, Ellery thought with a sigh. She hadn't. Manor houses, it seemed, were all too available, and Maddock Manor was in enough disrepair to make developers turn away. At least they hadn't been pestering her. 'No, not really. We're a bit off the beaten track.'

Larenz nodded slowly. 'I'm amazed Amelie found this place, actually.'

Ellery bristled; she couldn't help it. 'I do have a web-site—'

'Mmm.' Larenz pulled at the canvas tarpaulin. 'If I'm not mistaken, there's a car under here, and probably a nice one.'

Ellery's heart seemed to stop for a second before it started beating with hard, heavy thuds. 'A Rolls-Royce,' she confirmed as Larenz pulled the tarpaulin away to reveal the car. They gazed silently at the vintage vehicle, its silver body gleaming even in the dim light. Ellery wished she'd taken Larenz to another barn. She'd forgotten the car was kept in this one. Actually, she'd forgotten about the car completely, yet now she found the memories rushing back and she reached one hand out to touch the gleaming metal before she dropped it back to her side.

'A Silver Dawn,' Larenz murmured. He ran his hand over the engine hood. 'From the nineteen-forties. It's in remarkably good condition.'

'It was my father's,' Ellery said quietly.

Larenz glanced at her. 'Has he passed away?'

She nodded. 'Five years ago.'

'I'm sorry. You must have been quite young.'

'Nineteen.' She gave a little shrug; she didn't want to talk about it, especially not with Larenz, a virtual stranger. She didn't like talking about her father to her closest friend. She certainly wasn't about to unburden herself to a man like Larenz.

'You could sell the Rolls,' Larenz commented as he covered the car back up; Ellery felt a sudden pang of loss. She'd ridden in that car as a child, stuck her head out of the window and laughed with joy as her father had motored down the narrow country lanes, waving at everyone who passed.

She'd also stood on the front steps and watched the Rolls disappear down the drive when her father had gone on his alleged business trips. She'd never known when he would be coming back.

'Maybe I don't want to sell it,' she said, her voice coming out in something of a snap.

Larenz glanced at her, unperturbed. 'It must be worth at least forty thousand pounds.'

Forty thousand pounds. Ellery had no idea the car could be worth that much. She felt foolish for not knowing and yet, even so she knew she would never sell it. Another emotional and irrational decision, but one she couldn't keep from making. She turned away, walking stiffly out of the barn. 'Some things aren't for sale,' she said quietly after Larenz had followed her out and she had closed the big wooden door, sliding the bar across.

'Forty thousand pounds would make a big difference to a place like this,' Larenz remarked mildly. 'You could mow the lawn a bit more regularly, for starters.'

Ellery whirled on him, suddenly furious. 'Why do you care?' she demanded. 'You've been here less than twenty-four hours. You already think my home is a wreck. And,' she added, real bitterness now spiking her words, 'I don't recall ever asking you for advice.' She turned on her heel—her boots splashing through a rather large puddle and, she noted with satisfaction, spraying mud onto Larenz's jeans—and stormed back to the house without once looking back at her guest.

# CHAPTER THREE

BACK at the house, Ellery rinsed off her boots and lined them up on the stone step outside. Anger still pulsed through her, making her hands tremble as she opened the back door. She was angry with herself for being angry with Larenz; he wasn't worth the emotional energy she'd already wasted.

Not to mention her physical energy. It was late morning and she hadn't dealt with the breakfast dishes, or made the beds, or done any of the half-dozen demands that required her attention on any given day.

Stupid, arrogant Larenz de Luca had completely thrown off her day, she thought furiously. He'd thrown more than her day off; he'd unbalanced her whole self, making her see Maddock Manor in a way she tried not to. She kept herself so busy working and trying and *striving*—all for something she knew she could never gain or keep. And Larenz, with his expensive car and clothes, his smug little smile and knowing eyes, made her realize it afresh every second she spent in his presence.

What was even more aggravating was her body's treacherous reaction to a man she couldn't even like. She knew just what kind of man Larenz was, had known it from the moment he'd driven up the lane in his sleek Lexus and tossed the keys on the side table in the foyer as if he owned the place. She'd seen it in the careless way he treated his lover, Amelie, and the way she responded, with a distastefully desperate fawning. And, most damningly of all, she saw it in the way he treated her, with the sweeping, speculative glances and the lazy voice of amusement. He was toying with her and enjoying it. The fact that Ellery's body reacted at all—betrayed her—was both infuriating and shaming.

'I'm sorry.'

Ellery whirled around, her thoughts lending the movement a certain fury. Larenz stood in the doorway of the kitchen; he'd removed his boots and there was something almost endearing about seeing him in his socks. One of them sported a hole in the toe.

'You're sorry?' she repeated, as if the words didn't make sense. They didn't really, coming from Larenz. It was the last thing she'd expected him to say.

'Yes,' he replied quietly. 'You're right. I shouldn't be giving you advice. It's none of my business.'

Ellery stared at him; his eyes had darkened to navy and he looked both serious and contrite. The sudden about-face disconcerted her, made her wonder about her own assumptions. Now she was left speechless and uncertain, not sure if his words were sincere.

'Thank you,' she finally managed stiffly. 'I'm sorry, as well. It's not my usual practice to insult my guests.'

A smile quirked Larenz's mouth and his eyes glinted again, as sparkling and blue as sunlight on the sea. The transformation made Ellery's insides fizz, and she felt faint with a sudden intense longing that she could not, for the life of her, suppress. It rose up inside her in a consuming wave, taking all her self-righteous anger with it. 'I'm not really a usual guest, am I?' he teased softly.

'A bit more demanding,' Ellery agreed, and wondered if she was actually flirting.

'Then I must make up for my deficiencies,' he replied. 'How about I make us lunch?'

His suggestion caused another frisson of wary pleasure to shiver through her. Ellery arched her eyebrows. 'You can actually cook?'

'A few things.'

She hesitated. They were stepping into new territory now, first with the little flirtatious exchange and now with the idea of Larenz actually making lunch—cooking—for her. Dangerous ground.

Exciting ground. Ellery hadn't felt so alive in ages, not since she'd first buried herself here in the far reaches of Suffolk, and probably far before that, too. She sucked in a slow breath. 'All right,' she finally said, and heard the mingled reluctance and anticipation in her voice. Larenz heard it, too, or she assumed as much from the wicked little smile he gave her.

'Fantastic. Where are your cooking pots?'

Smiling a little bit, a bubble of laughter threatening to rise up inside her and escape, Ellery showed him where everything was. Within a few minutes he was playing at executive chef, dicing a few tomatoes with surprising agility as a big pot of water bubbled on the stove. Ellery knew she should go upstairs and make the beds, but instead she found herself perched on the edge of the table, watching Larenz move around the kitchen with ease and grace. He was wonderful to watch.

'How did a man like you learn how to cook?'

His shoulders seemed to stiffen for a single second before he threw her a questioning glance. 'A man like me?' he repeated lightly. 'Just what is that supposed to mean?'

Ellery shrugged. 'You're wealthy, powerful, entitled.' She ticked the words off on her fingers, not meaning them as insults although, from the still stiff set of Larenz's shoulders, she had the uncomfortable feeling that he took them as such.

'Entitled?' he repeated wryly. 'I'm afraid not. You're the one with the title.'

Was she imagining the bitter undercurrent in his voice? Surely she was. 'I don't mean an actual title,' she said. 'Useless as they are—'

'Are they?'

'Mine is.' She swept an arm to encompass the whole Manor, her whole life. 'It's just a courtesy anyway, because my father was a baron. Besides, what's good about being Lady Maddock, besides having to pay death in taxes?'

'Nothing is certain except death and taxes,' Larenz murmured as he minced two fat cloves of garlic.

'Exactly.' Ellery paused, both unable and unwilling to voice how this new side to Larenz had surprised and even unsettled her. 'Men like you don't usually learn basic life skills,' she finally said.

'Men like me,' he echoed thoughtfully. 'And that's because someone is always doing it for us, I suppose?' He paused in his slicing and dicing. 'Fortunately, my mother had a more prosaic view. She made sure I learned all of life's necessary skills.' He slid her a sideways smile that did strange things to her middle; it was as if something were opening and closing inside her, like a fist.

'I see,' Ellery murmured. She felt herself blushing, her whole body heating from just a single look. Suddenly the kitchen felt very warm.

'We can eat as soon as the pasta is done,' Larenz told her. 'No more than a simple tomato sauce, I'm afraid. My skills are indeed basic when it comes to the kitchen.' Yet his playful emphasis suggested that his skills were both more advanced and adept outside of the kitchen.

Such as in the bedroom.

Or was that where her own desperate thoughts were taking her? She was mesmerised by the way his hands moved so quickly and skilfully as he prepared their lunch; she watched the sunlight play on his dark curls as he bent his head to his task and felt nearly dizzy with need.

She needed to stop this, Ellery told herself. She had no intention of getting involved—in any way—with Larenz de Luca. She might feel a brief and admittedly intense attraction for him—intense simply because she'd denied her body for so long—yet she had absolutely no interest in acting upon it. She couldn't.

The thought of being intimate—vulnerable—with someone like Larenz actually made her shudder. She would not be beholden to a man like Larenz de Luca, a man who would surely turn his back on her without a second thought. A man who, by all evidence, treated women as playthings, as amusements. And surely he was merely amusing himself with her in an effort to while away a long lonely weekend. Was that why he had stayed? For his own bored amusement? Surely the supposed business proposition was no more than a pretext.

Larenz peered into the pot. 'I believe it's done.'

Ellery forced her thoughts—and their natural direction—away. 'Isn't it supposed to stick to the wall?' she asked, half-teasing, and he grimaced.

'Foolish folk tales. An Italian knows when the spaghetti is done simply by looking.'

'Where did you grow up in Italy?' Ellery asked. It was an impulsive question, breaching the wall she'd erected between servant and guest. Tearing down the self-defences she'd made despite her resolve not to be involved. Interested.

Yet somehow she kept asking the questions, somehow she stayed. Her mind and body were clearly at war.

Larenz drained the pasta and ladled it into two bowls before replying. 'I'm originally from Umbria,' he finally said. 'Near Spoleto, but really in the middle of nowhere.'

'Your family is still there?' Ellery asked.

Another pause. She felt as if the questions were becoming intrusive, although she'd meant them to be innocuous. 'Not any longer,' Larenz finally answered, and brought the bowls to the table. 'Now let's eat.'

He'd placed the bowls on one end of the table, leaving Ellery little choice but to sit next to him instead of her earlier, safer place at the far end. It would surely be offensive—and obvious—to move her bowl to the other end of the table.

Still, Ellery hesitated and Larenz glanced at her, clearly amused. 'I don't bite, you know. Unless asked, of course.'

Ellery rolled her eyes. 'Oh, please.' She sat down and, from the fleeting little grin he gave her, she knew he'd been outrageous on purpose; it had, strangely, put her at ease.

They ate for a few moments in a silence that was surprisingly companionable. Larenz's knee occasionally pressed against hers, and Ellery wondered if it was accidental. He seemed unaware of the times when they touched, although surely he could see how those brief brushes affected her? Several layers of fabric separated their skin and yet, every time his knee pressed against hers, her whole body tensed as though preparing to resist an assault.

And it was an assault, an onslaught of the senses, for each time he touched her she felt her body—and her resolve—weakening further. She felt pleasure and need flood her body, overwhelm her senses, so that she couldn't think about anything but the purely physical joy of being touched.

She wanted this. To be touched, desired, loved, even if it was only for a moment's amusement.

*No.* The realization was far too shaming. She could not allow herself to think this way. Feel this way. Yet her body disagreed; every nerve blazed to life, every sinew singing with reawakened awareness. Her body wanted more.

And so her body betrayed her. Without being even fully cognizant of what she was doing, she moved her foot so it brushed against Larenz's leg. She felt taut muscle under her toes. He didn't even pause, and Ellery felt a ridiculous flaring of disappointment. What on earth was she doing? Was she actually playing footsie under the kitchen table?

And the most galling part was Larenz didn't even notice.

Maybe he really hadn't meant to touch her, the brushing of their knees no more than an accident. Perhaps his attraction, just like her own need, was all in her head. In her body, now stirring to life with suppressed longings and taking over her common sense. Larenz looked as if he felt nothing at all. And while that should relieve her—keep her safe—Ellery discovered, to her annoyance, that it simply made her feel frustrated.

He raised his head to smile at her, and Ellery knew she'd been caught staring. She turned resolutely back to her pasta. 'So tell me about this business proposition of yours, if there really is one at all.'

'You doubt me?' Larenz asked, sounding amused. Ellery shrugged. 'As a matter of fact, I own a chain of department stores—De Luca's.' He raised an eyebrow. 'You've heard of them?'

Ellery nodded. Of course she'd heard of them; there was a De Luca's in nearly every major European city. She'd hardly call it a department store, though. It was too upmarket for that. She certainly couldn't afford anything there. She supposed she should have made the connection earlier, when she'd learned what Larenz's last name was. Yet, even though she'd known him to be rich, she hadn't quite realized just how powerful and wealthy he truly was.

He really was slumming here, staying at the Manor, flirting with her. Amusing himself, and that only a little.

'Amelie scouted your Manor for a fashion shoot,' Larenz continued. 'The shoot will launch a new line of haute couture I've commissioned, and I'd like it to be done here.'

Ellery stared at him in disbelief, her lunch—and even

her longings—momentarily forgotten. 'You want to stage a fashion photography shoot here?'

Larenz smiled, steepling his fingers under his chin. 'Is that so strange?'

'As a matter of fact, yes. There are dozens—hundreds—of manor houses in this country, houses that are in better shape than Maddock.' It hurt to say it, even though it was glaringly obvious. 'Why would you choose a third-rate place?'

He was still smiling that faint mocking little smile that drove her just about crazy. Ellery bit the inside of her cheek. 'You don't think much of your home.'

'I'm honest,' Ellery returned flatly. 'Something I don't think you're being.'

'Maddock Manor has a certain…ambience…we'd like for the photo shoot.'

Ellery stared at him for a full minute, trying to grasp what he was saying. She was missing something, she was sure of it, because there was no way one of Europe's most elite stores would want to market their new high-end fashion label at a falling-down wreck of a house in deepest Suffolk. Was there? She narrowed her eyes. 'This is pity, isn't it?'

'Pity?' Larenz repeated questioningly, as though the word was unfamiliar to him. Before Ellery could make any kind of reply, he reached over and touched his thumb to the corner of her mouth, pressing lightly against her skin.

Ellery's lips parted instinctively and she heard her breath escape in a tiny, soft sigh that betrayed her utterly. Larenz's smile deepened and he murmured, 'You had a bit of sauce there.'

Ellery felt a flush burn its way up her body, right to the roots of her hair. She'd always blushed easily and she hated it especially now, for surely Larenz saw how he'd affected her—how he'd meant to affect her, touching her so provocatively.

Or perhaps it hadn't been provocative; perhaps he'd merely

been wiping away a dab of sauce, and she'd read more into it because she was so desperate with longing.

She rose from the table, reaching for the dishes almost blindly and bringing them to the sink, her back to Larenz.

'Ellery?' he asked, his voice mild yet questioning.

Ellery dumped the dishes into the sink and watched almost impassively as a bowl broke cleanly in half. She hated how confused she felt, sensuality and self-protection warring within her while Larenz seemed completely unaware of the pitched battle going on.

She heard him rise from the table; she sensed him standing close behind her, felt his heat and his strength. She even inhaled the now familiar tang of his aftershave. 'Why are you doing this?' she asked in a low voice. She realized she no longer cared if she embarrassed herself. She needed to know why. Was he even aware of how much he affected her? Surely he had to be. Surely he was enjoying this little game.

'Doing what?' Larenz asked. His voice was carefully bland.

Ellery turned around. 'Teasing me,' she said, her voice still low. 'With this ridiculous business proposition, with—' She swallowed, unwilling even now to admit how much his careless little touches and flirtations affected her. 'Are you amusing yourself for the weekend because your lover left early? Since nobody else is available, you've decided I'll do?' The accusations poured out, scraping her throat raw. 'I don't need your pity, Mr—'

He pressed a finger to her lips, silencing her. 'You think I pity you?'

'I know you do.' She drew in a ragged breath; his finger was still on her mouth, and she tasted the salt of his skin. 'I see it every time you look around this place. You think it's a hovel, a mouldering wreck like your...your *mistress* called it last night!' Ellery was breathing hard and fast now;

she was angry, angrier than the situation merited, and she knew why. Larenz reminded her of her father. Larenz treated Amelie—and her—like her father had treated her mother. Someone to take or leave, as he desired, with no regard for the sorrow or heartbreak he caused. Fresh rage poured through her.

'Amelie is not my mistress,' Larenz said calmly.

Ellery snorted in disbelief, despite the ridiculous lurch of hope she felt at his words. He had to be lying. 'You really expect me to believe that?'

He gave a negligent little shrug. 'I suspect you will believe what you will. I confess I had no idea you were making such assumptions about me. But, in point of fact, Amelie is the head of public relations for my company. That's why she was here at all, trying to find a place suitable for the fashion shoot—'

'You cannot expect me to believe that anyone finds this place suitable.'

'Obviously you don't.' He dropped his voice to a lulling whisper. 'Why are you here, Ellery? Why do you stay? I wonder if you even like this Manor of yours very much.'

Ellery recoiled. The questions were too revealing, too close to the truth. She was not about to answer them, or give Larenz any more information that his sense of perception had already gained him.

She tried to turn away but his finger was still against her lips, and now he touched her chin, forcing her to look at him.

'Ellery, I do not pity you. I must admit, I would find it hard going to take care of this place on my own as you do, but that hardly translates to pity.'

'When it sounds, looks and feels like pity, it generally is,' Ellery retorted. She tried to jerk her chin away from Larenz's grasp but he held on, smiling as he dipped his head so their faces—and lips—were no more than a breath apart.

'I assure you,' Larenz murmured, '*this* isn't pity.' And, before Ellery could process or protest that statement, his lips met hers and he was kissing her in a way she'd never been kissed before.

He was kissing her in a way that made her forget every resolution or regret she'd ever had.

Ellery remained unmoving under his caress for the briefest of seconds; she was too dazed to do or think anything, her mind and body both frozen with surprise. Then her senses took over, flooding with sweet, warm pleasure, and her body spurred into action, responding of its own accord, without the permission of her still-resistant mind.

Her arms came up and twined around Larenz's shoulders, her fingers splaying across the taut muscles of his back, her head falling back and her body arching, as sinuous and sensual as a cat. She heard herself make a sound she never had before, part of her incredulously aware of how wanton she was being. She moaned, the sound trembling on her lips, reverberating through her body.

Larenz deepened the kiss.

His hands had drifted down her back and now cradled her hips, drawing her closer to him, the contact intimate and revealing. His hand moved upwards to stroke her breast through the thin fabric of her T-shirt, his lips still on hers, tasting and exploring, and the sudden nerve-tingling jolt the caress caused made Ellery stumble back, coming hard against the sink.

The moment, hazy with desire, had now turned crystal-clear with cold reality. Ellery felt sick and when she swallowed she tasted the acidic bite of bile.

'Don't—' she whispered. Her heart thudded as if she'd run a mile and her whole body still tingled with the aftershocks of his kiss.

Larenz smiled. Besides his hair being a bit rumpled,

he looked remarkably composed. 'Don't what?' he asked pleasantly. 'Don't stop?'

'Don't tease me,' Ellery burst out. 'Don't toy with me.'

For a moment Larenz looked genuinely nonplussed. 'Why am I toying with you, Ellery?' She liked how he said her name, the trace of an accent in the caress of the syllables. 'I want you. You want me. Really, it's very simple.' His expression hardened for a single second as he added, 'It doesn't have to be difficult.'

She shook her head. She felt her throat clog and her eyes fill damningly with tears. She couldn't speak without giving herself away, so she bit her lip—hard—instead. It wasn't simple at all. Not to her, at least. Yet she could hardly explain that to Larenz, especially when she barely understood it herself. All she knew was that giving herself to a man like him now—like this—would not be the simple physical pleasure he seemed to think it would.

It would, Ellery knew, be the selling of her soul.

She shook her head again, managing to get one word out of her constricted throat. 'No,' she said and, pushing past him, she fled from the room.

Larenz stood in the quiet of the kitchen, trying to process the last few minutes. What had started so promisingly had ended, he realized ruefully, rather disastrously. Ellery Dunant had looked, damn it, near to tears. Had such a simple little kiss really affected her so deeply, so terribly?

It didn't bode well for his planned seduction.

Moodily, Larenz wandered to the bank of windows that overlooked the walled garden. Sunlight made the puddles shimmer, and the dew-spangled grass looked as if it were gilded with silver. There was a strange, almost ethereal beauty to the Manor grounds, and Larenz could see why Amelie had thought it would be such a spectacular backdrop for the new couture gowns De Luca's would be showcasing next spring.

Ellery was a bit like her beloved Manor, he thought with a philosophical bemusement. She shrouded herself in plain clothes and unflattering hairstyles but she still couldn't hide the beauty underneath, the beauty he saw in her bruise-coloured eyes and elegant bone structure. And not only beauty but desire; he'd seen it in the way her eyes darkened to storm clouds, the way her body had trembled and yielded to his when he'd kissed her.

He hadn't even meant to kiss her right then. Leaning against a kitchen sink was hardly the most comfortable place for seduction. Yet in that moment when he'd felt the velvety softness of her lips against his finger—skin on skin—he hadn't been able to think of anything else. Want anything else. Kissing her hadn't been an indulgence; it had been a necessity.

Larenz expelled his breath in a frustrated sigh. Yet what had that kiss been to Ellery? Judging by her response, he would have thought it an awakening. Yet, remembering the shattered look in her eyes as she'd fled from the room—and from him—Larenz wondered if it had, instead, been, bizarrely, a betrayal.

He pushed the thoughts aside. He didn't want to wax philosophical about an insignificant little kiss; he certainly wasn't going to *care*. All he wanted was a weekend of pleasure and if Ellery Dunant couldn't handle that then he'd leave her damn well alone.

She was, Larenz decided firmly, nothing special. And, since he didn't mix business with pleasure anyway, he should just forget all about her. Go and pack. Move on. He was good at that.

Yet still he remained staring out at the unkempt garden and in his mind's eye all he saw was the hurt flaring in Ellery's violet eyes.

# CHAPTER FOUR

ELLERY didn't see Larenz for the rest of the day. After she'd run from the kitchen like a frightened girl—shame and anger warring within her—she'd gone upstairs to deal with the dirty sheets. She needed to work, to do and not to think. She needed to regain some balance and some common sense.

Yet she found neither when she stepped into the Manor's master bedroom, with its tangled sheets and the cold ashes of a fire in the grate. Ellery sagged against the bedpost, her mind replaying the images she'd envisioned last night—Larenz and Amelie in that bed, before the fire…

Firmly she pushed such thoughts away—along with the accompanying absurd jealousy—and stripped the sheets from the bed. An expensively cloying perfume she recognized as Amelie's drifted up from the sheets. Ellery grimaced.

She bundled them into a pile to take downstairs to the rather ancient washing machine, another appliance on the brink of collapse, stopping only when she saw the door to the room next to Amelie's was ajar. She kept the doors to all the bedrooms firmly closed in a somewhat futile effort to maintain some warmth in the main sections of the house.

Now she stepped inside, gazing around in surprise at the neatly made bed; a pair of shoes—men's dress shoes—were lined up at its foot. The bag Larenz had carried in last night was on the divan by the window and she could see his woollen trench coat hanging in the wardrobe.

Had Larenz slept here? Had he and Amelie had a fight? Or had he actually been telling the *truth*?

Ellery took a step closer to the bed and reached down to smooth the faded counterpane. Then, on impish impulse, she bent and sniffed the pillow. It smelled of a citrusy aftershave. It smelled of Larenz.

Ellery straightened. She felt strangely unsettled, relief and uncertainty mixing uncomfortably within her. She also knew she did not want to be caught snooping in Larenz's room. Quickly she backed out of the bedroom and hurried to pile the sheets in the washer.

Yet all afternoon vague unsettled thoughts drifted through her mind like wispy clouds, insubstantial and yet still greying her day. Had she misjudged Larenz? What kind of man was he, really? She wondered just how much of her assumptions had been based on her own experience and how much on what she saw and heard from the man himself.

'So he had a fight with Amelie,' she muttered as she went to the kitchen to see about dinner. 'He slept in another room, and she flounced off in a huff. It doesn't change anything.' It shouldn't change *her*.

Kissing a man like that—*wanting* a man like that—still felt like a betrayal of who she was and every hard lesson she'd learned from another betrayal—her father's.

The sun had started its descent and the gardens were already cloaked in dusky shadows. Larenz had left earlier that afternoon, speeding off in his Lexus, and he still hadn't returned. Ellery had no idea if she should make a proper dinner or settle for her usual tinned soup or beans on toast. Yet if Larenz did return, he would undoubtedly expect a meal. The thought of waiting on Larenz alone in the huge, shadowy dining room made nerves leap low in her belly.

She pushed the feelings aside and made herself a cheese

sandwich, eating it alone at the kitchen table as darkness claimed the grounds. Although she lived alone for most of the year, tonight she was especially conscious of the empty house all around her, still and silent, room after cavernous room yawning into infinity.

Ellery snorted in disgust at her own fanciful thoughts. She was getting maudlin again. She could go down into the village, visit a fellow teacher from the secondary school where she taught part-time. Get out of the Manor, and out of her own head. Yet she knew she wouldn't. She was too restless, too wary. And, she acknowledged ruefully, she was waiting for Larenz to return.

She stood up abruptly and put her dishes in the sink. A gust of wind rattled the windowpanes and the boiler started clanking again.

She thought of Larenz's knowing questions that afternoon: *Why are you here, Ellery? Why do you stay? I wonder if you even like this Manor of yours very much.*

The questions pointed to a grim truth: sometimes she hated this house. She hated the memories made here that caused her to doubt who she was; she hated that she stayed because this house felt as if it was all that was left of who she was. She hated how her life was sucked into taking care of its empty rooms and endless repairs, and yet the thought of giving it up—selling her only home—was akin to selling her soul.

Just like kissing Larenz had been.

Ellery groaned. 'Stop it,' she said aloud. Living alone, she was used to talking to herself. Yet the words had little effect. She couldn't stop thinking about that kiss, or how it had reached deep down inside her and shaken up all her longings and fears until she didn't know which was which. She couldn't stop remembering how it felt to be held in Larenz's arms, to have his lips on hers, to feel touched and treasured and dare she even think it—loved.

Ellery didn't consider herself enough of a dupe to imagine

even for a second that love had anything to do with what Larenz wanted. It didn't have anything to do with what *she* wanted.

Love was dangerous. Frightening. Forbidden. Especially with a man like Larenz.

No, all she wanted—all she could want—was a moment, a night of pleasure like Larenz had promised.

So why had she hightailed it like a scared rabbit or, more appropriately, a shy virgin after her first kiss? Why couldn't she enjoy what Larenz offered? Why couldn't she take what he offered without feeling afraid or, worse, used? Betrayed?

Why did it have to mean anything?

Tired of the questions that ran around in her head in useless circles, Ellery left the kitchen. There was still plenty for her to do: paperwork and paying bills, not to mention the general housekeeping she'd neglected for much of that day. The downstairs reception rooms needed a good dust and polish, and she'd been slowly—very slowly—plastering some of the cracks in the walls of the foyer. Yet her endless DIY list held little appeal as she wandered from room to room, wondering just how—and when—the house she'd once adored as a child had become an impoverished prison.

Of course she knew the answer, even if she didn't like to think about it. It had started when her father had chosen to live two lives rather than one.

Larenz pulled up in front of Maddock Manor and groaned aloud. Under the sickly glow of a waxy moon the place looked even more decrepit than usual. He'd spent the afternoon driving around the country, motoring down narrow twisting lanes and through quaint sleepy villages—what had he been looking for? Another place for Amelie's photo shoot? Or had he just simply been trying to forget?

Forget the look in Ellery's eyes when he'd kissed her.

Forget the feeling of her in his arms—fragile, precious, unforgettable.

Of course he couldn't forget.

Even a whisky at the local pub—the man behind the bar had been particularly closed-mouthed when Larenz had casually asked about Lord Maddock and his damned Manor—had only blunted the raw edge of desire that had been knifing through him all afternoon.

Muttering a curse, Larenz slammed the door of his Lexus and stalked towards the Manor. He stopped halfway to the front portico for a light had flickered in the corner of his vision, somewhere in the gardens behind the house.

Larenz's mind leaped ahead to intruders, thieves, murderers, rapists. He thought of how isolated Ellery Dunant was here, mouldering in her Manor all by herself, and when he saw the light flickering again—it looked like a torch in someone's hand—he swung around and began to stalk towards the barns.

'Damn it to hell,' he said aloud, for he knew his earlier determination was shot to pieces. He did care.

Ellery pulled the tarpaulin off the Rolls and stared at it under the sickly yellow glare of her torch. She let her breath out slowly; funny how even after years stored in a barn the car still retained its gorgeous gleam. Funny too how she'd almost forgotten it was here, how she'd made herself forget.

Until Larenz had forced her to remember.

Slowly she let her hand run along the antique car's mudguard. The metal felt like hard silk under her fingers. Without even realizing she was doing so, she let out a small choked sound that was far too close to a sob.

Damn her father for making her love him so much. Damn him for hiding so much from her. Damn him for dying, and damn him for making her the kind of woman she was now, alone and afraid to love.

Damn. Damn. Damn.

Ellery lifted her hands to swipe at the revealing moisture at the corner of her eyes. She drew in a desperate breath and let it out again; she needed to regain some composure, some control. Ever since Larenz had breezed into her life—just a little over twenty-four hours ago—she felt as if both had been slipping away from her. Why did he affect her so much? Why did she let him?

She let out another long, slow breath and then resolutely covered the Rolls back up. Perhaps she would sell it. Forty thousand pounds would, as Larenz had said, go a long way.

As she turned towards the barn door, feeling her way with careful slowness, the pale beam of the torch barely cutting a swathe through the unrelenting darkness, she wondered where he was. Was he coming back? Had he breezed out of her life as quickly and easily as he'd breezed into it, simply because she wasn't the easy affair he'd counted on?

Why was she disappointed?

Then every thought flew from her head as a body tackled her, slamming her hard against the barn door, and the torch fell from her hand.

Ellery didn't realize she'd screamed—and was still screaming—until a hand covered her mouth. Even in the midst of her terror and shock she was conscious of a familiar citrusy scent.

*'Larenz?'* she said, the words muffled against the hand still covering her mouth.

She heard what could only be a curse muttered in Italian. The hand dropped from her mouth, and she saw Larenz bend to pick up the torch. He shone it in her face, and she squinted in the sudden light.

'What are you doing—'

'What are *you* doing,' Larenz demanded, his voice sounding almost raw, 'out in the barn at one o'clock in the morning? I thought you were a thief—or worse.'

'And you didn't think to ask questions first?' Ellery retorted. She rubbed her shoulder, which had hit the door hard. She would most certainly have a bruise.

'Where I come from, you ask questions second,' Larenz said roughly. He shone the torch up and down, inspecting her body. Ellery was uncomfortably aware that she was wearing her dressing gown and wellies. Not the most enticing combination. 'Are you all right?'

'A bit bruised,' she admitted. 'Didn't you consider I might be inspecting my own property?'

'In the middle of the night? No.' Larenz paused, the torch still trained on her body. 'I'm sorry. The last thing I wanted was to hurt you.'

Ellery stilled, surprised and even moved by the contrition in Larenz's voice. 'It's all right,' she said after a moment. 'I was about to go inside, anyway.'

She started to move away from the door but Larenz stilled her, one hand on her shoulder. 'Ellery, why were you out here? Were you looking at the car?'

Ellery heard a note in his voice she didn't like, couldn't like. It was the gentle note of compassion, and it spoke of a song she couldn't bear to hear. Tears stung her eyes and she blinked them furiously away.

'Perhaps I am thinking of selling it,' she said roughly and pushed past him.

She couldn't make her way in the dark without stumbling and possibly even hurting herself more so Ellery was obliged to wait for Larenz to catch up. Silently, he handed her the torch and she took it with stiff dignity. They walked back through the muddy gardens without speaking.

Once in the kitchen, Ellery shed her boots and went automatically to the big copper kettle on the range. She desperately needed a cup of tea, or perhaps something even stronger.

'You should ice your shoulder.'

She stiffened. 'It's really not necessary.'

'I slammed you rather hard against the door,' Larenz replied evenly. 'If you don't ice it, it will bruise.'

'I can handle a bruise.'

'Why are you so touchy?' Larenz murmured. That sleepy, hooded look Ellery was beginning to know well—and to both dread and desire—had come into his eyes, turning them a deep glinting navy. 'Besides, I know for a fact there's a big bag of peas in your chest freezer. I saw it last night when you so thoughtfully fetched me some ice.' He smiled and Ellery's heart turned over. Or squeezed. Or something, making it suddenly rather hard to breathe.

Larenz moved to the freezer, opening it and rifling through the contents before emerging with a bag of peas. 'There. Plonk that on your shoulder for a bit.'

It would be easier, Ellery knew, to simply give in. If she iced her shoulder for a few minutes, perhaps then Larenz would leave her alone. Although half of her—more than half—didn't want him to leave her alone. A good, and growing, part of her wanted him to stay…and more. So much more. She couldn't deny the insistent need spiralling deep within her, pushing away any thoughts of regret or betrayal.

She swallowed and looked away. 'Fine,' she said and grabbed the bag of peas, pressing it against her shoulder. It was hard to do without wrenching her other shoulder, not to mention looking entirely awkward and, seeing this, Larenz took the bag from her. 'Why don't I do it?' he murmured.

'No—'

'Are you worried I'll kiss you again?' His words were no more than a breath against her ear as he leaned down to press the bag of peas against her shoulder; his head was bent so his jaw was no more than a whisper away from Ellery's own lips.

And, just like that, the mood in the room changed, awareness replacing annoyance, the atmosphere more charged than ever before.

'I wouldn't say worried,' Ellery managed. She moved her head back, away from the temptation of Larenz's skin. Her heart slammed against her chest and her mouth had turned bone-dry. She was conscious of Larenz's breath feathering her cheek. No, she wasn't worried. She was wanting.

Wanting him.

She felt desire pool languidly in her limbs, felt her body and mind soften and open into possibility. At that moment she didn't know why Larenz affected her so much, why her body responded in such a basic and overwhelming way to his. She didn't care. All she knew was that she did want him to kiss her again, and more, and she was so very tired of fighting it. Her body acted of its own accord, leaning into him, her senses straining once more for his touch. He was so close; she could brush her lips against the warm, rough skin of his jaw and it would practically be an accident...

The kettle began to whistle shrilly, and Ellery jerked back as if it had actually scalded her. The bag of peas fell to the floor, splitting open so the peas rolled everywhere.

Larenz glanced down in bemusement. 'Oh, dear.'

Ellery turned off the stove, her back to him, her blood and heart pumping far too fast. That had been close. So very, very close...

'Why were you in the barn, Ellery?'

'Would you like a cup of tea?' She turned around, the tin of tea held to her chest like a shield.

Larenz smiled and shrugged. 'I don't usually have tea at this time of night, but why not? Especially if there is a drop of brandy to go with it. You could use some, I'm sure.'

'There's a bottle somewhere,' Ellery mumbled, turning back to the kettle. Larenz moved closer.

'Why were you in the barn?'

'I told you, I was checking up on things,' Ellery replied stiffly. She reached for two mugs and her hand trembled. 'Why do you care?'

Larenz didn't answer for a long moment—long enough for Ellery to pour the tea and hand him his mug. She stared at him, surprised at the way his eyes had darkened with shadows, the angles of his face suddenly seeming harsh.

'I don't know why I care,' he finally said thoughtfully. 'I've been asking myself that all evening.'

Ellery felt that curious squeezing sensation in her chest once more and for a few seconds it was difficult to take a breath. She rummaged in a cupboard for the requested brandy. 'I think it's here somewhere…' She was so very conscious of Larenz behind her, of the tension tautening between them and uncoiling in her own belly. She was conscious of her own rising need; the intervening moments had not stemmed it. She still felt. She still wanted.

She tried to keep her voice light as she asked, 'Where were you all afternoon? Did you go touring?'

'You could say that. I drove.'

'Drove where?' The conversation was utterly inane and made even more so by the fact that she didn't care what his answers were. Speaking was simply a way of keeping herself from doing something far more desperate—and desirable.

She finally found the brandy in the bottom of the pantry, the bottle dusty but the amber liquid still glinting in the light. 'Here you are.'

Larenz took it, his fingers wrapping around the neck of the bottle and over Ellery's own hand. His gaze locked with hers, dark and unrelenting, and every thought flew from Ellery's head. She was trapped by that gaze and she had the strange sensation that Larenz was as trapped by it—by this—as she was. Ellery didn't move. She couldn't. She knew if he kissed her now she wouldn't resist. She wouldn't want to.

And why should she? She'd been locked up in this Manor,

keeping it like some kind of shrine to a family, a life that had never really existed, for six long months. She wanted to stop, if only for a night. Stop thinking, fearing, hiding.

And start living. Larenz was here, his eyes were on hers, his lips parted, his expression hungry and intense, and suddenly Ellery knew exactly what she wanted.

This.

She let go of the bottle, not thinking of it or anything but her own need and the answering look in Larenz's eyes, and somehow it slipped, shattering at their feet. Yet neither of them even reacted to the broken glass and spreading liquid, the pungent smell of alcohol rising up towards them. Something far more dangerous was happening.

Ellery didn't know who kissed who first. She didn't care. All that mattered was that she'd found her way into Larenz's arms and he was kissing her, his lips hot and hungry on hers as her arms wound around his neck, her fingers threading through his hair as she pulled him closer, and closer still— how she needed this...

'The glass—'

'I'll clean it up later,' she mumbled, turning her head to find his lips once more, eager and greedy. She felt Larenz smile against her mouth.

'I prefer not to need to have stitches,' he murmured, and in one easy graceful movement he'd swept her into an embrace, carrying her out of the kitchen and up the Manor's sweeping staircase. He held her easily, as if she were weightless, and Ellery felt like a doll in his arms, small and treasured.

'Where's your bedroom?' he asked, and then shook his head. 'On second thoughts, forget it. If your bedroom was anything like mine last night, I don't want to go there.'

'Worse,' Ellery admitted.

'What's the warmest place in the house?'

Ellery's heart squeezed again. Yes, she wanted this—she really did—but, now that the heated moment in the kitchen had cooled just a little, she was left wondering and afraid once more. Just what was she getting herself into? 'The master bedroom, I suppose,' she answered after a moment, 'or the drawing room when the fire is on—' Her voice wobbled just a little bit. Ellery closed her eyes in embarrassment.

'You're getting cold feet, aren't you?' Larenz placed her back on the floor so her body slid sensuously against his, his hands still on her shoulders, until her feet touched the ground. She swayed towards him and he reached up to tilt her chin with one finger so she was forced to meet his gaze. 'Ellery?'

'Not cold,' she corrected with a shaky laugh as her gaze slid away from his. 'A bit cool, perhaps.'

She felt rather than saw his smile, and they stood there in the dark and quiet, the house full of empty shadows all around them, the only sound their own breathing.

It took Ellery a moment to realize that Larenz was not speaking on purpose; he was not trying to convince her with words or, far more persuasive, with kisses. He was giving her time. He was letting her decide.

Slowly she leaned in and rested her forehead against his chest; he slipped his hand down and laced his fingers with hers. They remained that way, silent and swaying, for several moments. A thousand thoughts tumbled through Ellery's head. She realized she had no idea what she was doing...or why. She was afraid and excited and, strangely, a little sad. Yet she also knew if she could stretch this moment out into eternity, she would. She'd be happy just standing here in the dark, touching Larenz, feeling his breath and his heat, his hand gently—so gently—squeezing hers.

He wasn't the man she'd thought he was. The realization slipped into her mind slyly, like a secret, yet a good one. She'd assumed Larenz de Luca was an entitled, womanizing bastard—and yes, he'd seemed like it at first—but, even so, Ellery knew she'd leaped to conclusions because she was afraid. Afraid that any man who touched her—touched her heart—might turn out like her father, leaving her as brutally betrayed as her mother had been. Leaving her alone.

She'd never been willing to take the risk.

Yet Larenz had shown her too many small, surprising kindnesses for her to rest on her assumptions. To hide behind them. And right now she didn't want to. Right now she wanted to forget…and to feel.

She tilted her head upwards, her eyes still closed, and found Larenz's lips with her own. Her kiss was no more than a brush, but it served as an answer to the question Larenz's silence had posed.

*Yes.*

His arms came around her and he pulled her against him; Ellery went unresisting, without trepidation or fear.

'Come with me.'

# CHAPTER FIVE

ELLERY followed him back downstairs, his fingers laced with hers as he led her through her own house, walking with the confidence of a man who knew exactly where he was going. And Ellery followed without needing to know where, or why. Now that she'd made her decision, she felt strangely, surprisingly at peace; she was content to rest in the moment, in being with Larenz, without jumping ahead to the what-ifs or why-nots.

He led her to the drawing room with its huge marble fireplace, now lost in shadow, the only light a gleam of lambent silver from the moon high above, visible through the gap in the heavy curtains at the windows.

'I assume this fireplace works?' Larenz said. He'd slipped his hand from hers and now crouched in front of the hearth.

'Yes, although I usually just use the electric—'

'This?' Larenz unplugged the three-bar electric fire she'd placed in the great old hearth with obvious contempt. Ellery found herself smiling. The electric fire had been sensible, or so she'd thought; she kept the firewood for guests. Yet now she found she was pleased as Larenz reached for the birch logs piled up next to the fireplace and began, quite expertly, to lay and then light a fire.

Within a few minutes a comfortable, friendly blaze was

crackling away, the flames casting long orange shadows around the room and over Larenz's face, making him look a little devilish. A little dangerous.

'Things getting cool again?' Larenz teased softly, and Ellery couldn't help but laugh, in spite of her lingering nerves, for he'd read her perfectly.

*He knows me so well.* The thought was ridiculous, absurd, for of course Larenz de Luca didn't know her at all. She'd only met him yesterday. Yet Ellery couldn't keep herself from thinking it—and perhaps even believing it.

'Come here,' Larenz said.

He was kneeling in front of the fireplace, his face half in light, half in shadow, and his voice sounded both teasing and a little raw.

Ellery went to him.

She stood in front of him, a little uncertain, a little breathless. Larenz tugged at her hand, and she dropped to her knees in front of him. The logs crackled and shifted, scattering some sparks across the carpet. Larenz brushed it with his fingers.

'We can't ruin another rug of yours,' he murmured, and Ellery tried to smile. She felt so nervous.

'At least this one's not an Aubusson.'

'You know all the antiques in this house of yours?' Larenz asked. His hand slipped along the nape of her neck, his fingers rubbing her tense muscles.

'Yes…my mother catalogued everything in this house.' Ellery's breath hitched. She was finding it difficult to concentrate with Larenz's deft fingers on her. 'She left a list… I went over it when I first came back.'

'How long ago was that?'

'Six months. My mother was going to sell this place and I couldn't—' She stopped suddenly, her throat tight. Larenz finished the thought for her.

'Couldn't imagine life without Maddock Manor in it somewhere?'

'Something like that.'

'Where is your mother now?'

'In Cornwall.' Ellery managed a smile. 'She lives in a lovely little thatched cottage and is happier than she's ever been.' Happier than she'd ever been with her father, Ellery added silently. She was glad her mother had found her place, her peace. She just needed to find hers.

She didn't want to talk any more, not about her house or her history, and Larenz must have sensed that for he smiled and reached to take the clip from her hair.

'I've been wanting to see your hair down ever since I first met you.'

'All of twenty-four hours ago?' Ellery joked, but it came out a bit flat.

'It's been a very long twenty-four hours,' Larenz replied and he released her hair.

Ellery almost always wore her hair pulled up any which way; it was more practical and there was never anyone to impress. Now she felt surprised by her own sensual response to the fall of her hair as it shimmered about her face and shoulders in a pale cloud. She shivered when Larenz threaded his fingers through it, his thumb brushing her cheek and the fullness of her lip.

'Beautiful…just as I imagined. Or perhaps better. You look like The Lady of Shalott.'

'You know that poem?' Ellery asked in surprise, for Tennyson's ballad was one of her favourite poems.

'You know it was based on an Italian story? *Donna di Scalotta*. I like the English version better, though.' He quoted softly, '"There she weaves by night and day, A magic web…"' He brushed his lips against her jaw. 'You've certainly woven some kind of magic around me.'

Ellery thrilled to his words, even as another more logical part of her was insisting that surely she was not like that doomed lady, isolated and imprisoned in her island castle, pining for the handsome Lancelot. Surely, unlike the sorrowful Lady of Shalott, she had a surer hand in her own destiny—and a happier fate.

Then all thoughts fled Ellery's dazed mind for Larenz was kissing her again, his lips moving slowly over hers, exploring every contour as he pulled her closer, and closer still, and she surrendered herself completely to the caress.

She wanted to forget. She wanted to feel. To feel and not to think.

Larenz's hands slid along her nightgown, deftly undoing the row of buttons down the back. 'I dreamed of you wearing something like this,' he murmured into her neck. 'Yards and yards of white flannel… I can hardly wait to unwrap you.'

Ellery gave a shaky laugh. 'It keeps me warm.'

'Good thing I lit a fire,' Larenz replied and gently pushed the nightgown off her shoulders. The garment slid from her body, landing in a heap of cloth, which Larenz kicked aside. All Ellery wore was a pair of thick woollen socks. She was uncomfortably conscious of her own nakedness, even though in the dim light, her body bent, her hair hanging down, Larenz could hardly see her. Yet she couldn't help but notice that he still wore all his clothes.

'This feels a little uneven,' she said, trying for a teasing note, and Larenz cocked his head, his eyes gleaming in the half-light.

'So it does. How should we remedy the situation?'

And Ellery knew exactly how. Smiling a little bit, emboldened by her own desire—and Larenz's—she reached for his T-shirt. 'I think I can help.' She pulled the T-shirt from his torso while Larenz obediently raised his arms, watching her with a sleepy half-smile. His chest gleamed bronze in the firelight and Ellery sucked in her breath. He was a beautiful man. And tonight he was hers.

Cautiously, she reached out and touched the taut muscle

of his chest, letting her hand drift down to the waistband of his jeans. And there she stopped.

She glanced back at his face and saw him watching her with a knowing—and almost gentle—little smile. Her fingers played with the button of his jeans. She let out a little ragged laugh.

'Shall I help?'

'I'm a bit…new…to this.' It was as close as she was willing to admit to just how new she was.

Larenz's hand covered her own and, emboldened once more, Ellery undid the button.

Just a few seconds later he'd been divested of all his clothes—and Ellery of her socks—and they were both naked, stretched out in front of the fire, the flames casting dancing amber shadows over their bodies.

Larenz ran a hand along her calf, to her thigh and then her hip, before cupping the fullness of her breast. 'You're beautiful,' he said with such sincerity that Ellery felt tears come to her eyes.

She didn't believe him. Couldn't. She was nothing special—blonde hair and odd-coloured eyes and an average body. She didn't want Larenz's platitudes or sentiments aimed at seduction; she couldn't stand lies.

She turned, covering his mouth with her own to keep him from speaking, her arms twining around his body as she pressed closer to him and felt her own feminine softness come up against his hard chest and thighs. Larenz responded, deepening Ellery's desperate kiss, his hands roaming over her nakedness and, as Ellery closed her eyes, she let pleasure take over, stealing through her veins like a drug, blotting out all remembrance and regret.

It was all too easy to give herself up to the moment, to let her body's need take precedence over her mind's fear, and as Larenz caressed her, kissing and touching and loving every inch of her body, Ellery writhed and moaned and cried out his name, her fingernails snagging on the worn carpet, her mind blissfully blank.

A moment came when Larenz hesitated, his body poised over hers. 'Are you protected?'

'Nnn…no,' Ellery stammered, thinking of her heart. Her heart was all too dangerously exposed, and yet of course Larenz meant her body. He rolled off her, rifling through his clothes, and Ellery felt a pang of something that was halfway between hurt and disappointment.

'You were prepared.'

'Let's say hopeful,' he murmured, slipping on the condom he'd taken from the pocket of his jeans. Ellery pushed all her thoughts away and gave herself up to pleasure once more.

She experienced a brief flicker of pain as Larenz pushed past her innocence, and she heard his own sucked-in breath of surprise. She closed her eyes and pushed back, opening herself up to him, and after a tiny second's pause Larenz embedded himself deeply inside her, groaning against her lips in both need and satisfaction. Ellery felt the flickers of pleasure blunt the pain in both her body and heart, and then the flickers turned to waves that crashed over in a tide of satiation and the pain was—for the moment—utterly obliterated.

Afterwards, they lay in a tangle of limbs, their skin golden in the light of the few dying embers left in the grate. Larenz traced circles on her skin with his fingertips as Ellery laid her head against his shoulder.

'You should have told me you were a virgin,' he said. Although he spoke in a lazy, sensual tone, Ellery sensed a different undercurrent. Disappointment, perhaps. She tried not to tense. Had she not been a good enough lover?

'I didn't think it was important,' she said with a little shrug. Her virginity, strangely perhaps, had not even crossed her mind when she'd considered whether to give herself to Larenz. It had been her heart and soul's safety and innocence she'd been more concerned about, rather than her body's.

Larenz's fingers stilled on her skin. 'A woman's first time is always important. If I'd known—'

Ellery propped herself up on one elbow, daring to look down at Larenz's brooding face. 'You would have taken more care? Or perhaps you wouldn't have bothered in the first place?'

He let out a sigh that wasn't an answer at all. 'I just wish I'd known.' Gently, he pushed Ellery's head back down on his shoulder and, as she resettled herself, his fingers stroked her temples. Ellery closed her eyes. She suddenly felt almost sleepy.

'I didn't think it really mattered,' she said after a moment. 'I decided I wanted you, and that was it.'

'Oh, was it?' Larenz teased, sounding amused. 'And here I was thinking I was the one who decided I wanted you.'

'Well,' Ellery said, barely suppressing a yawn, 'I suppose it was mutual.'

'Yes, indeed, *dormigliona*.'

She laughed a bit and snuggled deeper into the silken warmth of his shoulder, content to lie there for ever in Larenz's half-embrace.

Yet they remained like that for a moment, no more, and then in one deft movement he rose, scooping her up and taking her with him. Ellery was too sleepy and sated to do anything but curl into him and let him take her where he would.

Larenz strode through the darkened empty rooms of the Manor, naked and magnificent, and upstairs to the master bedroom, which Ellery had laid with fresh sheets only that afternoon. He peeled back the satin duvet and laid her on the bed. In the darkness she could not read his expression or even see his face, but Ellery smiled up at him, waiting, expecting him to slide into the bed next to her and take her in his arms once more.

He didn't.

He hesitated, or seemed to, although in the darkness Ellery couldn't be sure. Then he bent and brushed a kiss on her forehead. As his lips grazed her skin, he whispered, 'Sweet dreams, my Lady of Shalott.' And then, before Ellery could even draw a breath, he was gone. She heard the click of the door closing and then the sound of Larenz's footsteps down the hall.

Alone in the darkness Ellery was conscious of the cold slippery sheets against her naked limbs and, far worse, the coldness creeping inside her, stealing straight to her heart. Why had Larenz left so suddenly?

Yet, even as she asked herself that question, Ellery knew the grim answer. Tonight had been simply that: a night. And now it was over.

She never should have expected a single thing—or a single moment—more.

Minutes before, she had been content to drift into a satisfied sleep but now, lying there, she felt cold and unhappy and most definitely awake. She rose from the bed, grabbing one of the complimentary dressing gowns she'd hung in the wardrobe herself, a rather cheap attempt to make Maddock Manor more upmarket than it was or ever could be.

Enveloped in thick, rough terrycloth, she stole downstairs, not wanting to alert Larenz to her presence. Yet he wasn't downstairs; he seemed to have disappeared completely. Ellery half-wondered if he'd actually left the Manor itself, and that brief kiss had been her only goodbye.

She forced the thoughts away, keeping her mind determinedly blank. Yet, as she entered the drawing room and saw their scattered clothes and the ashes of the fire Larenz had laid, she heard the raw tearing gasp of her own pain. Wrapping her arms around herself, she took several steadying breaths and then turned to go to the kitchen.

She needed that cup of tea.

Yet the abandoned mess in the kitchen told its own

sorrowful story; the scattered peas and shattered glass glared at Ellery as she stood there, silent condemnations of her own folly. She drew another breath; it sounded like a shudder, halfway to a sob.

She set her chin and threw her shoulders back as she went for the broom and dustpan. None of this, she told herself, should come as a surprise. This was what she'd expected, even wanted, when she'd allowed herself to kiss Larenz. A night of pleasure, a chance to forget—for a moment.

Now she was just dealing with the remembering. And the regret.

Ellery bent to her task of cleaning up the mess in the kitchen, allowing the menial nature of the chores to numb her mind and keep the thoughts at bay.

She'd risen to empty the dustpan in the rubbish bin when she caught sight of her face in the darkened windowpane. Her face was ghostly pale, her hair streaming over her shoulders in a pale river. Just like the doomed Lady of Shalott. Then, unable to stop herself, Ellery let the tears trickle slowly down her cheeks.

Alone in his bedroom, Larenz let out a moody sigh, the sound entirely at odds with the sleepy satiation stealing through his body.

Yet, even as his body tingled and remembered and longed for more, his mind was coldly listing all the reasons to walk away from Ellery Dunant right now.

Tonight had been a mistake. A big one. He chose his bed partners carefully, made sure they knew exactly what to expect from him: nothing. Nothing beyond a night of pleasure, maybe a week. Yet when Ellery had snuggled into his arms, when he'd felt the way she'd fitted so perfectly, he'd realized she would expect a good deal more than that. He'd felt it in her soft, pliant body, in the satisfied little sigh she'd given.

In the fact that she had been a virgin. Larenz hadn't expected *that*; she had to be in her mid-twenties at the least. Yet she'd chosen to give herself—her innocence—to him? On the floor of her own wrecked home?

Larenz turned away from the window, unable to deal with or even accept the scalding sense of shame that poured through him. He didn't bed virgins. He didn't take them on the worn floors of their ancestral homes.

He didn't break their hearts.

Yet, alone in his bedroom, conscious of the creak on the stair, Larenz realized he might have done just that. Or he would, given time. He had no intention of sticking around for Ellery Dunant to fall in love with him, to think of him as Sir Lancelot to her tragic Lady of Shalott. There was no happy ending to that story, and there wouldn't be one here, either. Larenz knew very well that happy endings like the one Ellery was undoubtedly envisioning didn't exist. He knew it from the hard reality of his own life, his own disappointments… and he had no intention of experiencing that kind of rejection again. He would never give himself the opportunity.

Yet, even as he made these resolutions, his face set in grim lines, Larenz couldn't quite keep his mind from picturing Ellery's violet eyes, from his body remembering how soft and silken she'd felt in his arms. And he couldn't keep both his mind and body from wanting more.

Ellery Dunant was a luxury—and a liability—he couldn't afford. Resolutely, Larenz closed his mind from thinking about her. From remembering how she felt in his arms. Even so, sleep remained a long way off.

# CHAPTER SIX

THE next morning Ellery awoke to bright sunlight and a hard, glittering frost covering the ground. She rose from the bed, groggy and dazed. She must have slept, although she did not feel like she had. She certainly did not feel rested.

She fumbled for her clothes, trying to shake the fog that enshrouded her since Larenz had left her last night. She told herself she had no reason to feel this way; she had surely expected no more. She shouldn't feel *hurt*.

Dressed, her hair pulled into a tight bun—no Lady of Shalott for her this morning—Ellery headed downstairs. She had no idea whether Larenz would expect or even want breakfast, but she had every intention of keeping this morning as normal as possible. Even if the very idea made something inside her shrivel.

She paused on the threshold of the kitchen; all vestiges of the evening before had been cleaned away by her own hand just a few short hours ago. The kitchen suffocated her with its normality, for it looked as if nothing had changed. As if *she* hadn't changed. Yet Ellery knew she had; she felt it in the slight soreness between her thighs and the far more persistent ache in her heart. She hadn't expected that.

With grim determination she set about cracking eggs and slicing toast. She wondered if Larenz would even come downstairs. Had he gone? The house echoed emptily around her.

She wouldn't think about him, she told herself. She wouldn't think about him at all. She'd fill her mind with the trivial details of her day, with the to-do lists and DIY worries that had occupied her until he'd come into her life—there, she was thinking about him again. Ellery groaned aloud.

She left the eggs bubbling on the stove and went to fetch the two pints of milk the local dairy delivered every other day. As she opened the kitchen door, the sunlight hit her in the face, a brilliant yet cruel reminder that nothing had really changed over the course of one night, even if she had; if anything, the weather had just got better.

'Good morning.'

Ellery whirled around, the pints of milk clutched to her chest nearly sliding from her suddenly nerveless fingers. She tightened her grip and swallowed dryly. Larenz stood in the kitchen, dressed in a navy-blue suit, a coat hanging over one arm. He was, Ellery knew, coming to say goodbye.

Larenz gazed at Ellery, the milk clutched to her chest, the sun creating a golden nimbus around her cloud of pale hair. She looked like something out of a Constable painting, with the sunlight pouring in from the half-opened kitchen door, the wild gardens and crumbling brick wall visible behind her.

Her eyes were wide and shocked, the same colour as the shadowed circles underneath them. Of course, she couldn't have got very much sleep last night. Neither had he.

Still, despite his resolve to leave this morning, leave this woman and all her unnecessary and unwanted complications, he found himself now standing there, speechless, a growing tightness in his chest. Ellery looked so lovely, so fragile and yet with an inner strength he knew she possessed, radiating out from her despite the hurt and pain hiding in her eyes.

He'd hurt her. This was what happened when you opened

yourself up to anything more than brief physical pleasure. You got hurt. He'd taken something from her, something precious, and he would hurt her now, by leaving. Even if he didn't want to hurt her…even if he didn't want to leave.

Even if the thought of leaving hurt *him*.

'Good morning,' Ellery replied. She aimed for a brisk tone and just about managed it. She kicked the door closed behind her and put the milk in the fridge. She tried to think of something to say, but even the usual banal inanities seemed loaded with meaning: *sleep well*? didn't have quite the right ring. 'It's a beautiful day out,' she finally said, now sounding perhaps a little too brisk. She turned to the eggs; they'd overcooked and gone rubbery. 'Would you like the full fry-up this morning?'

Larenz hesitated and Ellery braced herself. Of course he didn't want a full breakfast, she told herself furiously. Not like yesterday morning, when he'd asked her to share his breakfast, when she'd still been an interesting and unknown challenge. Now he just wanted to leave.

'If you're making it,' he finally said, his tone neutral, but Ellery heard pity.

'If you'd rather just have coffee,' she told him with a bright, rather glittering smile, 'that's fine. The eggs look a bit overcooked, anyway.'

Smiling faintly, Larenz glanced in the pan. The eggs had congealed to its bottom. 'How about a compromise? Coffee and toast.' He paused. 'If you'll join me.'

She threw him a startled glance; he smiled, his face so very bland. How good he was at wiping away all expression, she thought resentfully. She had no idea what he was thinking, and she had an awful feeling that she was all too transparent. 'Very well.' She poured two mugs of coffee and fetched the toast. Larenz hung his coat over a chair and they sat across from each other, the awkwardness palpable, unbearable.

Ellery took a sip of coffee and burned her tongue. 'You're

off?' she enquired in that same awful brisk voice. 'I don't even know where you live. Are you returning to Italy or…' She let the sentence trail away for it occurred to her that perhaps he didn't want her to know where he lived. She hardly wanted to come across as some sort of stalker.

'I divide my time between Milan and London,' Larenz replied quietly. He hadn't touched his toast or coffee; he simply stared at her across the length of the table, his expression solemn now and perhaps even a little sorrowful.

Ellery took a bite of toast. It tasted like dust in her mouth. 'Sounds lovely,' she finally managed after she choked it down. 'Quite the jet-setting lifestyle.'

'Quite.' Larenz lifted his coffee mug, then placed it back on the table without taking a sip. 'You could come with me.'

Ellery stared at him, sure she must not have heard him correctly. 'Pardon?' she said politely, and waited to hear what he really must have said.

'You could come with me,' Larenz said again, and he sounded surprised, as though he hadn't expected to say it. Staring at him, Ellery was quite sure he hadn't.

She shook her head slowly, confusion and hope warring within her. 'Come with you? Where?'

'To London, and then to Milan,' Larenz stated matter-of-factly. He seemed to have recovered from his surprise. 'I have some business to do, but it could be…nice…to have company. It might do you some good, too. You don't have any guests booked for the next week or so, do you?'

'No, not yet,' Ellery said after a moment. The words *week or so* seemed to echo through her mind. Was that as long as this…affair…would last? 'I teach at the local school,' she added. 'But it's actually half-term this week.'

'Then why don't you come with me?' Larenz smiled and took a sip of coffee. 'You could use a break, I'm sure, and we could hammer out the details of the fashion shoot—'

'The fashion shoot?' Ellery repeated in disbelief. 'You still want to have it here?'

'Of course. My head of PR is quite set on this place.'

She shook her head slowly. The idea of a fashion shoot at Maddock Manor made no sense to her, but it hardly seemed relevant now. 'So you want to bring me to London and Milan to discuss business,' she said a bit flatly. 'Surely a week's trip isn't necessary for that.' She heard the slight edge to her voice as she added, 'You could just take me out for dinner.'

'I could,' Larenz agreed, smiling faintly, 'but this trip isn't about what's necessary.' He put down his mug and met her gaze directly, with an open honesty she hadn't been expecting, a vulnerability that reached right down inside her and grabbed her heart.

*No. Don't reach me. Don't touch me like that, with your eyes. Don't make me hope, don't make me fall—*

'I want you to come with me because I want to be with you,' Larenz said steadily. 'What happened between us last night—it was good.' He raised his eyebrows. 'Wasn't it?'

Ellery looked down. 'Yes, it was,' she whispered. It seemed such a simplification of the night they'd shared, not to mention the pain and sorrow she'd felt afterwards, but she could hardly voice that sentiment.

Larenz rose from the table, coming around to her side. He reached down and took her hand, tugging her upwards. Ellery didn't resist. She stood up, savouring his closeness, the scent of his aftershave, the heat and strength of him. He'd already become familiar. He laced his fingers with hers. 'Come with me, Ellery.'

'For a week?' she said, and Larenz paused.

'Yes.' He spoke steadily, flatly. 'That's all I have to offer.'

So those were his terms. A week, take it or leave it. A week, and then he would leave her for ever and she would return here, to the half-life she'd made for herself. Ellery knew she should say no. Agreeing would be opening herself up to all sorts of pain, hurt, sorrow. A week of being used, because surely that was all it was? A week was not a relationship.

She opened her mouth and yet still she didn't speak. The definite *no* didn't come. For, despite every logical reason to refuse, she still *wanted* to go. She wanted to escape this house and her life, and she wanted to be with Larenz.

'Ellery?' Larenz prompted gently, and she remembered how he'd let her decide last night. He'd waited then, and he was waiting now.

What if it didn't have to be like that? she wondered suddenly. What if she made these terms hers, instead of just Larenz's? She wasn't interested in love. She didn't even want a relationship; she'd kept herself from such things on purpose, out of self-protection.

What if *she* decided on a week's fling? What if she was in control?

The thought was powerful. Persuasive. Her mother had been at her father's whim, waiting hopelessly for his return, for his careless favour. Yet Ellery didn't have to be like that. She could take this week, enjoy it to the full, and when it was over she could be the one to walk away, her heart intact.

This, she thought suddenly, could be just what she needed. In so many ways.

She squeezed Larenz's fingers. 'Yes,' she said. 'I'll go with you.'

Larenz waited in the kitchen as Ellery went to pack. He felt restless, edgy and even a little hopeful. A strange mix. He had no idea why he'd asked Ellery to come with him to London. He'd had no intention of doing so; he'd been coming to say goodbye.

And then he'd found himself saying something else instead, and wanting it. Wanting her.

The thought was just a little bit alarming.

Of course, it didn't have to be. He'd made it very clear to Ellery what his terms were, what this week would mean—and especially what it wouldn't mean. And even if he'd broken all of his rules—bedding a virgin and mixing business with pleasure—he wouldn't break that one.

After a week, it was over. After a week, he would leave.

They left right after breakfast. It felt strange to pack a single case—she had few dressy clothes left over from her London days—and then to lock up the Manor, leaving it emptier than ever.

Larenz waited by his car; Ellery sensed his impatience, even though he didn't say anything or even glance at his watch. He was ready to go. To move on. And in another week, he'd be ready again. Well, so would she.

'Do you need to notify anyone?' he asked as Ellery slid into the front passenger seat of his car. 'I suppose things will just tick over for a few days?'

Ellery nodded. 'I was just planning on doing some maintenance around the house this week.' She smiled wryly. 'But I suppose it can wait.'

'Good,' Larenz said firmly and started the engine.

'It feels strange,' she admitted with a little laugh, as Larenz drove down the Manor's sweeping lane, 'to leave, even for just a little while.' She wanted to be clear that she understood the rules. That they were hers, too.

Larenz slotted her a quick sideways smile. 'It will do you good.'

Ellery stiffened. That was the second time he'd said that. 'Don't see this as some kind of mercy mission,' she warned him. 'I'm going with you because I want to. It's my choice.' She met his gaze directly. 'A week is all I want, as well, Larenz.'

Surprise flashed across his features, followed by what

could only be satisfaction. His mouth tightened. 'Good,' he said again, and just as firmly.

Ellery settled back in the seat, glad she'd made herself clear. *A week is all I want*, she repeated to herself, and she believed it.

They didn't speak again until they'd left both the Manor and village behind and the road stretched out in front of them, glittering under a bright autumn sun.

Larenz steered the conversation to more innocuous matters, talking lightly about films and books and even the weather; Ellery enjoyed chatting about such simple things.

'So you teach,' he commented as they turned onto the motorway. 'I can see you giving one of your stern looks to a classroom full of unruly boys.'

Ellery chuckled. 'Actually, it's an all-girls school. I taught full-time in London, but I gave that up when I came out here. Fortunately, I found a part-time job. One of the teachers was going on maternity leave.'

'And when she comes back? What will you do then?'

Ellery shrugged. 'I don't know. I don't have a long-term plan, to be honest.' She made herself smile. 'I know I can't hold on to Maddock Manor for ever.'

Larenz glanced sideways at her, speculative and a little compassionate. 'Then I suppose the question is—why hold on to it at all?'

'That is indeed a good question. I haven't yet found a good answer.' She stared out of the window at the trees lining their side of the motorway, their stark branches stripped of leaves and stretching towards the sky. 'Have you ever not been able to give something up, even though you know you probably should?' Larenz didn't answer, and so Ellery finished, 'That's how I feel about the Manor. I'm just not ready to let it go yet. All of my friends think I'm mad, of course.'

'Well,' Larenz said quietly, 'I think you're brave. Not

everyone is able to actually *do* something the way you have. Most people would just let it go and be sad.'

'Perhaps that's better.'

Larenz glanced at her again. 'Do you really believe that? Wouldn't you rather act and really live life than let it go by?'

Ellery swallowed, surprised by the intensity in his voice. Yes, she wanted to live life. She wanted to act. Wasn't that why she was here? She was taking control.

They lapsed into silence, and an hour later Larenz pulled the car up to the front of The Berkeley, an impressive-looking hotel in Belgravia.

He tossed his keys to the valet while a porter helped Ellery out of the Lexus. Larenz ushered her into the hotel's sumptuous lobby; she thought she saw a celebrity she recognized disappear into one of the exquisite dining rooms.

Ellery was breathless, overwhelmed by the luxury she had never experienced and yet should have expected. After all, Larenz de Luca was a wealthy, powerful man. And she was never more conscious of it than when he strode through the hotel lobby, the staff nodding and bowing to him. He was quite obviously a regular customer. The very idea that she was here with him seemed ludicrous, so much so that Ellery had to stifle a laugh of sheer amazement and wonder as she followed him through the sumptuous lobby.

'You come here often?' she asked as he gestured for her to enter the lift before him.

'I reserve a suite for my personal use,' Larenz replied with a shrug.

'Reserve?' Ellery echoed. 'You mean always?' The thought of paying thousands of pounds a night for a hotel suite to be on reserve seemed not only incredible but rather wasteful, especially in light of her own desperate financial situation. She could not imagine ever being so wealthy or privileged.

Larenz shrugged again. 'Not always,' he allowed. 'If I know I'm going to be out of the country for some time.' He gave her a knowing little smile. 'I'm not a spendthrift, Ellery. I didn't get to where I am by throwing money away.'

The statement, delivered in such a matter-of-fact manner, intrigued her. 'Get to?' she repeated. 'Where did you come from, then?'

The lift pinged and the doors whooshed open. Larenz gestured for her to enter the suite first. 'I told you before, near Spoleto,' he said lightly, but Ellery felt quite certain that he knew she'd really been asking something else.

Yet all thoughts of their conversation evaporated in light of the splendour of the suite Larenz reserved for his occasional use. Rooms stretched out in every direction, and Ellery silently marvelled at the polished marble and mahogany, the sumptuous carpets, the graceful Grecian columns that flanked the doors leading out to a private terrace.

She peeped in what was clearly the master bedroom and swallowed. 'It's gorgeous.' She'd become so used to the tattered state of Maddock Manor that the luxury and opulence left her nearly speechless. 'I can't believe I'm here,' she admitted with a little laugh.

Larenz came up behind her as she stared silently at the king-sized bed piled high with silk throw pillows and rested his hands lightly on her shoulders. Ellery shivered under his touch.

'I want you to enjoy it,' he murmured. 'Enjoy this. Let me spoil you, Ellery. I want to.'

His words caused a fingertip trail of unease to ripple down her spine. *Spoil* had such unpleasant connotations, she thought distantly, like rotting food. To be ruined, perhaps, for anything else.

Yet as she gazed around at the suite with its beauty and its finery, its handmade chocolates and a bottle of Krug champagne chilling in a silver bucket in the sitting room, she told herself that a week of being spoiled could do no harm...or at least not much. Surely she deserved a week out of time, out of reality. A week of this...and she wanted it. Just one week.

Whether it was right or wrong, good or bad, she wanted a week with Larenz. She wanted to be wined, dined, romanced and seduced. She wanted to be immersed in the wonderful whirlwind, to let it pick her up and take her where it would.

Eventually—in a week—she'd land with a thump, and when she did she'd go back to life, to reality, happy and satisfied. She *would*.

She turned around so she was facing Larenz and, with a little cat-like smile she'd never felt on her face before, she wound her arms around his neck. 'All right,' she agreed in a husky murmur as Larenz pulled her closer, 'if you insist.' And, by Larenz's answering smile, she knew he was pleased by her response.

They ate a late lunch of lobster bisque and caviar on crackers in their room, washed down with several glasses of champagne. By mid-afternoon Ellery was feeling wonderfully relaxed and even a little sleepy.

'I have to check in with a few things,' Larenz told her as a maid slipped in to clear their discarded dishes. 'But why don't you have a rest and a bath? We have reservations at the restaurant downstairs tonight.'

'All right,' Ellery agreed. Mentally, she went through the few clothes she'd packed and doubted whether the cocktail dress she'd worn to her college's May Ball four years ago would be elegant—or expensive—enough. Still, a rest sounded good; she was exhausted.

She stood in the centre of the suite's master bedroom with its huge king-sized bed piled high with pillows, its doors to the private terrace outside, and listened to Larenz moving through the living room.

Ellery slipped off her shoes and peeled back the satin duvet. As she slipped into the bed with its slippery sheets, she felt another shaft of amazement that she was here at all slice through her. A few seconds later she heard him speak in a low voice and knew he must be on the telephone. Who was he calling? What business did he need to check? Lying there, Ellery was forced to acknowledge just how little she knew her lover, her only lover.

Her lover for a week.

Her terms, she reminded herself fiercely. Those were her terms. It wasn't as if she was looking for *love*, and especially not from a man like Larenz de Luca: rich, entitled, uncaring. All he felt for her—could feel—was a brief physical pleasure; she *knew* that. She was not yet so desperate or deluded to think that anything would happen as a result of this week out of time, or that she even wanted anything to happen. She knew what loving someone—a man—did to you. She'd seen her mother wither and shrivel from her father's lack of love. Ellery didn't want that kind of life; she didn't want any man to have that kind of power over her. It was why she'd been a virgin until last night, why she'd avoided serious relationships at university and beyond, why even now she guarded herself from anything—or anyone—that could touch her heart. It was why she would end up alone.

But it was also why Larenz's offer of a single week suited her perfectly.

## CHAPTER SEVEN

WHEN Ellery awoke the sky was banked with violet clouds and the room thick with shadows. She heard a rustle of satin at the edge of the bed and she knew Larenz was there. She sensed him, smelled him and, when he rested a hand on her leg, she felt the comforting heat of him even through the thickness of the duvet.

'Hello, *dormigliona*.'

She snuggled deeper into the duvet; Larenz let his hand rove a little higher on her thigh. 'What does that mean?'

'*Dormigliona?* I suppose in English it would be sleepy-head. You've been asleep for over three hours.'

'Have I? Goodness.' Ellery sat up, self-conscious now that she was fully awake. 'I hardly ever nap. There's too much to do.'

'All the more reason for you to nap here,' Larenz replied easily. 'All you have to do is enjoy yourself.'

Ellery smiled and stretched under the covers. 'Sounds simple.'

'It is.' In the twilit dimness of the room she couldn't make out the expression on Larenz's face, but she was achingly aware of the charged atmosphere growing between them, the need spiralling deep inside herself. She leaned forward, expectant, waiting. Larenz removed his hand from her leg.

'I ran you a bath,' he told her as he rose from the bed. 'You didn't even stir when I came in here to do it, but I thought you'd like a nice soak before dinner.'

Ellery leaned back against the pillows, disappointment eroding her brief happiness. She'd wanted Larenz to kiss her, and more than that. She wanted to be in his arms again, to have him make her both forget and remember at the same time, in such a sweet, sweet mix of both longing and satisfaction...

'Come on,' he said lightly, 'it's getting cold.'

And then he left the room.

After a moment Ellery swung her legs over the side of the bed and pushed open the door to the en suite bathroom. A huge jacuzzi bath in sumptuous silvery-grey marble had been filled with fragrant foaming bubbles, a fluffy towel laid neatly on the side. Just the sight of that bath made Ellery feel every aching muscle; lukewarm showers and hot-water bottles back at Maddock Manor simply didn't compare.

'This hotel must have an amazing boiler,' she said aloud as she stripped off her clothes and a few seconds later sank gratefully into the silky, steaming water. She lay her head back against the marble and closed her eyes; she didn't know how long she lay there, relaxed enough to be in a half doze, when she heard the door open and her eyes flew open.

'Hello.' Larenz stood there, the sleeves of his crisp white shirt rolled up to his elbows.

Ellery sank deeper into the water, grateful for the foaming bubbles that hid her from view. Even though it was rather ridiculous to feel shy now, she still did. She wasn't used to this. She didn't even know how lovers were supposed to act. She barely knew how to flirt.

'I thought I could help you wash your hair,' Larenz said. He sat on the edge of the tub, and Ellery was conscious of both his nearness and her own nakedness.

'I don't—' she began, but Larenz smiled and shook his head.

'Trust me, it would be my pleasure.' He reached out to wipe a stray bubble from her cheek. 'Ellery, are you shy with me now? After what we've done—and been—to each other?'

Ellery shook her head as a matter of instinct. Yet the question Larenz had asked was a loaded one, and she wondered if he'd done it deliberately. Just what *had* they been to each other?

'All right,' she finally managed, scooting forward so he could access her hair, which she'd piled rather untidily on top of her head with a plastic clip. Realizing she sounded a bit grudging, she added, 'Thank you.'

Smiling, Larenz reached out and took the clip from her hair. It cascaded down her back in unruly waves, the ends trailing in the water. Ellery saw that Larenz had an arrested, almost mesmerized look in his eyes as he reached down and cupped his hands. She felt the pull of his gaze like a magnetic force between them, growing stronger in the steamy heat of the room. 'Lean back a bit.'

She did, conscious of how vulnerable she felt as Larenz cradled her head in the crook of his arm. She closed her eyes as he poured the warm water over her head until her hair was completely wet. He reached for the shampoo by the side of the tub and then began to lather her hair, his strong fingers massaging her skull and temples, eliciting a low moan of relaxed pleasure from her lips. His hands slid down to her shoulders, massaging those muscles as well, his thumbs skimming the top of her breasts.

'Time to rinse,' he murmured, and Ellery arched back so the water wouldn't get in her eyes, her head still cradled in Larenz's hands. She was achingly conscious of how intimate an experience this was, how it filled every sense with longing. 'Ellery…' On his lips her name was no more than a raw plea and Ellery's eyes flew open, stunned and gratified to know that he felt it, too, to see the flame of need turning Larenz's eyes to blazing sapphire.

Her lips parted but she couldn't think of a thing to say except, 'Kiss me.'

Larenz obeyed, leaning down to claim her lips with his own and Ellery's hands came up of their own accord, fisting the collar of his shirt, careless of how soaked he became.

The kiss went on endlessly, and yet it still wasn't enough. When Ellery felt Larenz lift his mouth from her own, she must have made some protest for he murmured, a sleepy laugh in his voice, 'I don't want to drown you.'

Easily, he scooped her up and carried her out of the bathroom, just as he'd carried her downstairs at the Manor. Ellery, wet and naked, curled into him; she'd never felt so safe, so cherished as she did in Larenz's arms.

Except, perhaps, for when he lay her down on the bed and gazed at her not with hunger, but with wonder. Something shifted inside her then; she felt her soul opening in a way it never had before, even when her body had yielded to his. Yet she didn't dare question just what it was she felt; the physical need was too great. And it had to be enough.

She reached up and twined her arms around his shoulders, bringing him to her, needing him near her, skin upon skin.

'Too many clothes,' she mumbled and, laughing, Larenz pushed away briefly to remove his clothes; his shirt was damp in patches from where he'd held her.

Then, as he returned to her and she felt the beauty and bliss of his skin on hers, their bodies aligned perfectly, no more objections—or even thoughts—came to mind.

Afterwards, they lay in the room, now nearly dark, their limbs in a satisfying tangle, when Larenz glanced at the clock and murmured, 'If we don't get moving, we're going to miss our dinner reservation.'

Larenz swung his legs over the side of the bed and was

now striding through the room, magnificently naked. Ellery watched as he threw open the doors of the wardrobe and reached for a crisp white shirt. She saw her own clothes had been hung up there as well, no doubt by the same maid who had cleared their dishes.

As Larenz began to dress, Ellery was strangely moved by the intimacy of the scene; they'd just risen from bed and were now dressing. It felt like something a couple would do, even a married couple, and the realization that they really were just two strangers made Ellery feel disconcerted, even disappointed, as if what they'd just shared was sordid rather than sweet. She pushed such thoughts away and rose from the bed.

'I'll just go dry my hair,' she said and, without turning around, Larenz nodded.

By the time she'd returned to the bedroom, Larenz had gone into the living room, although Ellery could still smell a faint citrusy whiff of his cologne. She dressed quickly, grimacing slightly at the rather plain black dress she'd brought. It was a classic, if rather inexpensive, LBD, which was why she'd bought it, but she'd realized afterwards that the cut was too severe and black made her look rather washed out. Sighing, Ellery pulled her hair into a chignon of sorts, not as tight a bun as she normally would have but still a severe hairstyle. She grimaced again. She looked like a disapproving housekeeper. At least her shoes were pretty: a pair of sparkly black open-toed stilettos she'd bought only a few weeks ago. She'd travelled to Ipswich to run errands and had seen them in a shop window. It had been an impulse buy and surely a ridiculous one, for she didn't usually wear heels and had no call to don a pair while living at Maddock Manor. Besides, they'd pinched her toes even in the changing room. Still, gazing in the mirror, she focused on her feet and decided any pain was worth it. They were fun, frivolous and entirely unlike her, but she loved them. And they gave her the courage to walk out of the room and into this strange—and amazing—new world.

Taking a deep breath, she headed out into the living room. Larenz turned around as soon as she entered, although Ellery had hardly made a sound. He looked magnificent in a beautifully tailored suit of grey silk and his gaze swept over her, taking in the plain unflattering dress, the severe hairstyle and ending at her feet. He smiled.

'Nice shoes.'

Ellery grinned. She couldn't help it. It was the best thing he could have said—the kindest and the most honest—and she gave a little laugh as Larenz's glinting gaze met hers and he smiled back.

'Shall we?' He held out his arm and Ellery took it.

'Yes.'

The restaurant was as opulent and luxurious as Ellery had suspected, yet on Larenz's arm the insecurities over her own attire faded to nothing. She was smugly conscious of the covetous looks a few women shot her, as well as a few curious and assessing glances by the men.

She felt like a movie star.

'The usual, Signor de Luca?' a waiter murmured, and Larenz gave a brief nod. Within minutes—seconds, even—the waiter had returned with a bottle of Krug and two delicate crystal flutes.

'I've never had so much champagne,' Ellery confessed after the waiter had left and Larenz raised his glass in a silent toast. She followed suit.

'I must admit, I am partial to it, especially when travelling. At home, of course, I drink only the best.'

'Which is?' Ellery asked, taking a sip of her champagne. The bubbles fizzed crisply on her tongue.

'Italian wine, of course. One of my interests is in supporting local vineyards. Drink up.'

Ellery took another sip; she had a feeling that on a rather

empty stomach the alcohol would go right to her head. Still, it relaxed her and surely that could not be a bad thing. All around her she heard the clink of crystal and the murmur of conversation. She glanced down at the menu, taking in the decadent offerings: caviar, truffles, filet mignon.

'So many choices,' she murmured, and Larenz glanced at her.

'Surely you've been to restaurants such as this before,' he said almost sharply. Ellery glanced up, surprised by his tone.

'Not really,' she said. She paused, wondering how much to reveal. How much she wanted to reveal. 'There wasn't much money growing up,' she finally said. 'The house is really the only thing of value we ever owned.'

'And the Rolls,' Larenz reminded her gently. He was looking at her with a shrewd compassion that seemed far too perceptive, too understanding, when Ellery reminded herself he didn't know anything about her. Not really. 'Tell me about him.'

The menu slid from her fingers. 'Who?'

'Your father.'

She shook her head too quickly. 'There's nothing really to tell.'

Larenz arched one eyebrow in blatant, if kindly, scepticism. 'There is always something to tell.'

The waiter had returned with a basket of flaky rolls and Ellery avoided Larenz's knowing gaze by devoting herself to selecting one. Yet, when the waiter had gone, the silence remained, and Ellery just shredded her roll onto her plate while Larenz waited.

'He was one of those people,' she finally said, her throat suddenly tight, 'who was larger than life. Charismatic, you know? Everyone loved him. He was everyone's friend, from the gardener to the greatest lord.' She looked up, smiled. 'My mother said she fell for his charm.' She stopped there because she didn't really want to talk about how her mother had realized that that was all she'd fallen for, how her father had deceived and destroyed them both, how hard it was to forgive, how even now she couldn't let anyone close. She found she just wanted to remember the good things.

'How did he die?' Larenz asked quietly.

'Cancer. It was very quick, just three months from diagnosis to—' She stopped again, shrugging.

'I'm sorry. It is hard to lose a parent.'

'You've lost one?' Ellery asked, for he spoke as though from experience.

Larenz paused, and Ellery knew he didn't want to tell her about himself, his family. God knew, she had her own secrets. Would it really surprise her that Larenz had some, as well? Yet she couldn't suppress a little wave of sorrowful longing that he didn't want to tell them to her, which was silly since she had not told him the whole truth either.

'My father,' he said at last. 'But I was not close to him. In fact, we were…estranged.'

'Estranged? Why?'

Larenz shrugged and took a sip of champagne. 'Why do these things happen? I could not say. It is only after—when it is too late—that you wonder if perhaps you should have been a bit more forgiving.'

They both lapsed into silence; Ellery found herself taking Larenz's words to heart. Should she have been more forgiving of her father? She'd only learned of his deceit upon his death, yet the truth had brought up so many painful memories, recollections of the times he'd disappeared, the birthdays he'd missed, the promises broken, the endless rounds of hope and disappointment, and all the while he'd been—

No. She wouldn't think of it. She didn't want the past to spoil the present, this one golden week. Ellery glanced down at her bread plate; her poor roll was no more than a pile of shredded crumbs. She pushed it to the side. 'Well,' she said, 'no use being gloomy. What do you suggest I order?'

'I'm partial to the wild sea bass,' Larenz replied, picking up his own menu and glancing at it, 'but the Angus fillet is very nice, as well.'

'I'll stick with steak,' Ellery decided. 'I'm afraid I'm not the most adventurous eater.'

'There are different ways to be adventurous,' Larenz murmured as he set his own menu aside. 'Coming with me for a week was certainly in the spirit of adventure.'

Ellery's cheeks warmed. 'Foolish, perhaps,' she said, and Larenz's eyes narrowed.

'Ellery, why do you say that? Do you regret your decision?'

She lifted her chin. 'No, of course not.' She smiled, keeping her tone light. 'But the house is going to go to rack and ruin in the week I'm away. I'd been planning to replaster the front hall this week, you know. I'd even gone out and bought the proper tools.'

'Very impressive,' Larenz murmured. His eyes danced. 'However, I have no doubt this week will be far more entertaining.'

Ellery pursed her lips thoughtfully. 'Well, I don't know. I was really looking forward to it, you know.'

Larenz laughed aloud, which made Ellery grin. He reached over and squeezed her hand. 'I love it when you smile. A real smile. You look far too sad sometimes.'

'I feel far too sad sometimes,' Ellery admitted quietly. The waiter came to take their orders before either of them could say anything more and she was glad. She'd said too much already.

'What made your mother decide to sell Maddock Manor?' Larenz asked eventually, his tone one of casual curiosity.

Ellery arched her eyebrows. 'You've seen the place, haven't you?'

He gave a small smile. 'Still, it's your ancestral home. Hard for her to let go of, I would think.'

'I suppose my mother had had enough,' Ellery said after a moment. 'She didn't have too many happy memories there.'

'You didn't have a happy childhood?'

Ellery shrugged. She didn't want to explain the endless cycle of disappointments, how her father's sudden, prolonged absences had affected her. 'Happy enough. But their marriage—' she took a breath '—went downhill after a while.' She took another breath, let it buoy her courage and met Larenz's gaze directly. 'That's why this suits me perfectly, Larenz. After seeing my parents' marriage fall apart, I'm not interested in relationships.'

Larenz didn't say anything for a moment, just watched her thoughtfully. 'Good,' he finally said and took a sip of champagne. He still gazed at her from over the rim of his glass. 'Because neither am I.'

'Good.' Ellery reached for her own glass. She felt wound up inside, everything held together so tightly, so tensely, and she couldn't explain why. Or why she felt just the tiniest bit disappointed. Hadn't they just cleared the air? Weren't they in agreement?

'You're an only child,' Larenz said after a moment. 'Aren't you? I haven't heard you mention any brothers or sisters. So I assume the line will die out with you?'

Ellery felt the tension twang inside her, ready to snap. Why was he asking *that*? 'Yes,' she said quietly, too quietly, 'I'm my parents' only child.' The silence ticked on for several seconds before Ellery forced herself to look at Larenz. He was studying her with a rather brooding expression, his brows drawn darkly together.

'Enough about me,' she said as lightly as she could, 'and my concerns. What about you? You said you were from Spoleto. Were you happy there?'

Larenz shrugged. 'I left Spoleto when I was five or six years old. I'm actually a city boy. My mother raised me in Naples, near her family.'

'And your father?'

Larenz paused, his expression turning obdurate. 'He wasn't in the picture,' he said flatly.

Ellery nodded, accepting, even though she wanted to ask about the sorrow his scowl seemed to be hiding, and why he didn't like the kind of probing questions he'd asked her any better than she did. She wanted to know more about Larenz, to understand him, yet she was also realistic enough to know that wasn't what this week was about. They were enjoying each other; that was all.

As the silence stretched between them, it suddenly seemed very little.

Ellery caught sight of the waiter heading towards them with two silver chafing dishes. She smiled at Larenz, throwing off the pall of gloomy remembrance that had briefly enshrouded them both. 'It looks like our starters have arrived,' she said lightly, 'and I for one am starving.'

They kept the conversation light for the rest of the meal, chatting about inconsequential matters, and yet even so Ellery felt as if neither of them had escaped the hold of the memories their earlier talk had stirred up. Certainly Larenz seemed a bit more preoccupied than usual, his expression sometimes distant and even dark.

By the time the dessert had been cleared and they both had refused coffees, Ellery was glad for the evening to be over. They headed back up to the suite in silence, each of them lost in their own thoughts.

Back in the suite, Ellery waited uncertainly in the living room; she had no idea what to do, having never been in such a situation before, and she couldn't read Larenz's mood at all. He'd shrugged out of his suit jacket and loosened his tie, but his back was to her and he hardly seemed aware of her presence.

She wished she could sashay up to him and take off his tie, smile sexily and head for the bedroom. She knew she couldn't. She simply stood there, as tongue-tied and uncertain as a teenager on her first date, wishing she knew the protocol. The expectations.

'Thank you for the lovely dinner,' she finally said.

'Of course. You know it's my pleasure.'

'All the same…' She trailed off, for Larenz had not turned around. He was staring out of the French windows at the view of Knightsbridge, although there wasn't much to see. The windows of the building opposite were dark.

Ellery stood there for several moments, hesitating, uncertain, before she finally—belatedly—caught on to the rather obvious signal Larenz was sending her. He wanted to be alone. Her presence, she acknowledged with a trace of bitterness, was no longer wanted or required.

Well, that was fine. *Fine.* She was still tired from her sleepless night and, in any case, they hardly had to live in each other's pockets all week. She was hoping to see Lil some time while they were here. It was fine if Larenz wanted to be alone. She could use a little space, too.

'I think I'll turn in,' she finally said, her voice stiff with dignity. 'Even with that nap, I'm rather tired.'

She turned around, heading for the bedroom and it was only when she'd reached the door, her hand on the door, that she heard Larenz's quiet, even sorrowful, answer.

'Goodnight, Ellery.'

Larenz remained where he was, facing the windows, for several moments. He heard the bedroom door close and then, more distantly, the sounds of Ellery getting ready for bed. He imagined her taking off that awful dress, kicking those decadent heels from her feet, the outfit as much a contradiction as

Ellery herself was. Beautiful and uncertain. Frightened and fierce. Brave and shy. He let out a ragged sigh. Even now he wanted to be in there with her, slipping the shoes from her delicate feet and tracing the bones of her ankles, sliding his hands higher…and yet he kept himself from following his base need.

A far more dangerous need had led him to do things he never did with a woman tonight: to ask questions, to want to know. He kept his lovers at an emotional distance for a reason. Larenz did not deceive himself about that. He didn't want them close because, inevitably, someone would get hurt, and he certainly didn't intend for it to be him.

Even now, he recalled his mother's defeated look whenever he'd asked about his father. He'd seen the pain in her eyes, had felt it in himself. And he remembered the blank, brutal look his father had given him, the one time he'd ever seen him face to face.

*I'm sorry. I don't know you. Goodbye.*

Muttering a curse in Italian, Larenz pushed open the doors to the terrace and stepped out into the cool, damp night. Why had he washed Ellery's hair? Why had he asked about her father? Why had he started an intimacy he professed never to want?

And yet, tonight, he *had* wanted it. He'd wanted to be with her, to know her secrets, to allay her fears. It was so unlike him, so unlike anything he'd ever wanted with a woman, and that couldn't be good. It alarmed him. Scared him, even, if he was to be honest.

He didn't like it.

He should never have asked Ellery along for the week, he reflected moodily. It had been a sudden impulse, the suggestion taking him by surprise as much as it had Ellery. He'd broken his rules in doing so, and he'd broken another one tonight. *Don't let them come close. Don't ask questions. Don't need.*

He'd seen it in her eyes this morning; she'd been expecting him to leave with a thank you and a goodbye. *He'd* been expecting to leave. His car keys had been in his hand. Why had he stayed? Why had he asked?

The answer, of course, was all too obvious. He'd wanted more—wanted Ellery—and a single night wouldn't satisfy. Well, that was fine; women had certainly lasted longer than a night. He'd been with several lovers for a month or even more. Yet, Larenz knew, that cold fear rippling unpleasantly through him once more, they'd lasted because they had been so undemanding, wanting nothing but physical pleasure and a few trinkets, tokens of his affection, which he carelessly gave away.

They didn't ask him questions, they never made him think. Want. Need.

Remember.

Ellery did. He didn't know how those clear violet eyes reached right inside him and clutched at his soul, made him want to tell her things he'd never told another person. When she'd asked about his father, he'd wanted to tell her about the fourteen-year-old boy he'd been, humbled, humiliated, *heartbroken* when his father had turned him away with a flat, forbidding stare. He'd never told anyone—not even his mother—about that. He'd never remotely wanted to.

He doubted Ellery was even aware of her effect on him. And while part of him longed to surrender himself to that want and need, to revel in it even, another larger part knew that would be the most dangerous thing to do.

He wouldn't do it.

He couldn't.

Larenz gripped the wrought-iron railings that surrounded the terrace and let a damp wind blow over him. Behind him, he saw the light in the bedroom wink out, and he imagined Ellery lying in that huge bed, uncertain and alone.

He'd go in there, he told himself, and make sweet love

to her again. He would do it to reassure her, and to reassure himself that physical pleasure was all they had. A week of pleasure, nothing more. Nothing less.

Wasn't that why he'd brought her along, after all? Yes, to get enough of her, but also to give her something. He'd felt bad—guilty—for taking her innocence so carelessly, a thoughtless seduction. A week of sex and spoiling, he'd thought, would assuage both his own sense of guilt and any sorrow she might feel over their union.

Besides, Larenz acknowledged with a bitter twist of his mouth, after a week she might get tired of mucking with the lower classes. *She* would tire of *him*.

Suppressing the sudden stab of fear that thought caused him, Larenz turned back inside. He headed towards the bedroom with cool determination, only to pause with his hand on the knob. From inside the darkened room he heard an alarming sound, something between a sniffle and a sob.

Larenz cursed again in Italian and whirled away from the door. He paced the living room, restless, anxious and half-wishing he'd never met Ellery Dunant.

## CHAPTER EIGHT

ELLERY woke suddenly, her eyes snapping open. All around her the bedroom was dark and silent. She had no idea what had awakened her but she was now achingly, painfully conscious of the smooth, empty space next to her in the bed. A glance at the clock told her it was two o'clock in the morning and Larenz still hadn't come to bed. At least he hadn't come to *her* bed; he might have availed himself of one of the many other beds in the hotel suite.

She lay there for a few minutes, the implications of this unwelcome possibility sinking into her. Why wouldn't Larenz come to her? This was her first night away with him. Could he have tired of her already? And, if so, why not just tell her to leave? That it was over?

Yet he hadn't. So, if he hadn't tired of her, what other reason could there be for keeping himself from her? Ellery found herself thinking back to their dinner conversation and how the questions about his past had sent him into a brooding silence. She didn't know what memories held Larenz captive; she only knew how painful her own were. Was it the regrets and remembrances of the past that were keeping Larenz from her now? Was he lost in unhappy memories, just as she'd been?

Knowing she could be horribly, humiliatingly wrong, Ellery decided to find out. She slipped from the bed, dressed only in the same fleece nightgown she'd worn at the Manor. She had no other pyjamas, much as she would have liked to don a silk teddy—if she even had the courage to wear such a thing.

She left her bedroom and tiptoed down the hall to the living room. A single light burned by the terrace and she saw Larenz sitting in an armchair, his back to her, his head bent.

Her heart turned over. He looked so serious, so intent, so… sad. Or was she simply being fanciful, jumping to conclusions based on her own earlier thoughts?

She crept closer, afraid to disturb him, yet yearning to talk to him, to touch him. She was behind his shoulder when she saw what had been making him look so serious.

'You're doing *Sudoku*?'

Larenz stiffened, startled, then swivelled slowly to face her. Despite his still-serious expression, Ellery felt a bubble of laughter rise up her throat; she managed to swallow it back down but she still felt a silly smile spread over her face.

'I'm sorry if I disturbed you.'

'No, no, I…I couldn't sleep.' She swallowed, for now that Larenz was facing her, she found he still wore an intense look that had nothing to do with his seemingly innocuous activity. She wasn't sure she wanted to know what it had to do with.

She let her gaze slide away from his and pointed to the top right grid of the puzzle. 'That should be a six.'

'What?' Surprised, Larenz turned back to his book.

Ellery leaned over his shoulder, one finger pointing to the page. 'That should be a six. See? You've made it a two, but it can't be a two because there's one already—there—' She tapped the number with one finger before withdrawing rather self-consciously. She'd wanted to keep things light, afraid of Larenz's intensity, but now she wondered if he would be annoyed or even offended. Some people were serious about their Sudoku.

Larenz stared at the puzzle for a long moment before he let out a chuckle. 'So you're right. You must be quite good at Sudoku to suss that out so quickly.'

'Well, I spend a lot of evenings alone.'

'By choice, though,' Larenz said quietly.

Ellery came around to the front of his chair, hesitating for only a second before she sat on the sofa opposite, her legs tucked up underneath her nightgown.

'Yes, by choice. I never thought living at Maddock Manor would be a social whirl.'

'Will your mother sell it one day?'

Ellery let out a slow breath. Sometimes she was amazed her mother hadn't insisted on selling it already. Even in its dilapidated state, the house was worth well over a million pounds. The very fact that her mother was willing to hold on to it made Ellery think she missed the happy times they'd once had, or believed they'd had, before her father had exposed it all as a sham. A lie.

'Probably,' she finally said. She glanced away, letting her gaze rest on the darkened silhouettes of the building opposite. Above them a pale slender moon glowed dimly through the clouds. 'I never thought I'd live there for ever.'

'Then what will you do when the place eventually goes?'

Ellery turned back to look at him rather sharply, wondering why he cared. Would it assuage his uncomfortable conscience, when he said goodbye, to know she had something ahead of her other than mouldering away at Maddock Manor? Was he pitying her? Was that why he'd brought her here at all?

The thought that she might be some sort of charity case was both humiliating and repellent. 'I suppose I'll go back to teaching full-time,' she said, injecting a cheerful, brisk note into her voice. 'I enjoyed it.'

'Did you? What did you teach?' Larenz was looking at her with that sleepy, heavy-lidded gaze that Ellery had come to know well. It meant she wasn't fooling him for a moment.

'English literature.' She gave him a pointed look. 'Including Tennyson's *The Lady of Shalott*. One of my favourite poems, although I don't think I like being compared to her.'

'Oh?' Larenz cocked his head to one side; if anything, his tone and look had become sleepier. 'Why not?'

'Well, she didn't have much of a life, did she? Imprisoned in her tower, only able to view life through an enchanted mirror, falling in love with Lancelot from afar, and he never even noticed her—'

'He did at the end,' Larenz objected softly. He quoted from the last verse of the poem: '"But Lancelot mused a little space; He said 'She has a lovely face—'"

'Not much, though, is it?' Ellery interjected, and heard the sudden bitterness in her own voice. 'Considering all she gave up for him.'

A silence descended that was both oppressive and awkward. Ellery had meant to show Larenz how fine she was by joking about that wretched poem, but she felt now she'd done the complete opposite. Annoyed, she glanced away.

'It's late,' Larenz said finally. 'You should go to bed.'

Ellery turned back to him, her eyebrows raised in challenge. 'Are you coming?'

Larenz hesitated. His gaze slid away from hers and Ellery's heart sank. 'Soon.'

She walked from the room in stiff silent dignity.

When she awoke the next morning, Ellery saw that the other side of the bed was still smooth and untouched. Either Larenz had not slept at all or he had not slept with her.

Determinedly ignoring the little painful pang this thought caused, Ellery rose from bed, showered and dressed. When she came out into the living room, she saw Larenz was already there, dressed in a business suit, a cup of coffee at his elbow as he scanned the day's headlines on his laptop.

'Good morning,' he said, barely looking up from his computer. 'There's coffee and rolls if you'd like. I'm afraid if you want the full fry-up you'll have to go downstairs.'

'Coffee is fine,' Ellery replied. She poured herself a cup from the cafetière and took a roll, still warm, from the basket before sitting down opposite Larenz.

They sat in silence for a few minutes, Larenz busy with his laptop and Ellery doing her best to sip her coffee with an air of insouciant unconcern. It looked to be a lovely day; bright autumn sunshine poured through the terrace doors and bathed the room in crystalline light.

'I'm afraid I have to go into the office today,' Larenz said. He glanced up from his computer briefly, his gaze resting on Ellery for only a few seconds before he turned resolutely back to the screen. 'A few things have come up that I have to deal with.'

'Nothing too serious, I hope,' Ellery replied. Her voice, she heard with relief, stayed light.

'No. Just the usual minor crises. But I hope you can amuse yourself for the morning?' He glanced up from the screen once more. 'I have accounts with most of the major stores here, as well as all the important designers. And of course, you can buy anything you want at De Luca's.'

'Of course,' Ellery murmured. She pictured marching into that sophisticated shop and asking for a boiler.

'So you should be all right? I'll be back after lunch, I hope.'

Annoyance streaked through her. 'I'll be fine, Larenz. I hardly need to be minded like a child. And as it so happens, I already have plans.'

'Oh?' Larenz hadn't moved or changed expression but he suddenly seemed wary and alert. Dangerous.

'Yes,' Ellery answered, courage firing through her. 'I used to live here, you know. I'm going to have lunch with one of my university friends.' She hadn't actually rung Lil yet, but she knew her friend would make time for her.

'Oh, really?' Larenz gave her an almost chilly smile. 'I hadn't realized you'd made such plans. What if I hadn't been busy?'

Ellery shrugged. It felt good to be in control for once. She'd agreed to this week because she thought she'd *be* in control, but she'd been spinning out of it ever since they'd arrived in London. It felt good to snatch a little back. 'I assumed you'd have business to take care of and, anyway, we can hardly be in each other's pockets all week, can we? From what I saw between you and Amelie, you don't particularly enjoy a clinging female.'

Larenz frowned, his eyes narrowing to navy slits. 'I already told you, there was nothing between me and Amelie.'

Ellery shrugged, refusing to argue. She wished she hadn't mentioned Amelie; the wretched woman hardly mattered any more. 'Even so.' She finished her coffee and rose from the table. 'You can't be cross I have plans, surely, when you've already said you'll be busy? Why don't we meet for afternoon tea downstairs? I read that The Berkeley puts on a good do.'

'*Tea?*' Larenz nearly spluttered. He sounded outraged.

'Or pre-dinner drinks,' Ellery suggested with a smile. 'You're right, I can't quite see you balancing a teacup and a scone.'

She turned towards the bedroom and, from behind her, she heard Larenz say tightly, 'Fine. We'll meet for drinks. But at least spend the afternoon shopping. I want you to wear something suitable this time.'

Ellery didn't answer. She'd tried for a light, unconcerned

tone to show Larenz she didn't care. She knew she wasn't meant to care, didn't even *want* to care, but he would never know how much it cost her. As she turned the knob of the bedroom door, her hand trembled.

Two hours later, Ellery stood in front of a soulless office building of glass and concrete in the heart of the city, waiting for her friend Lil to emerge. She was grateful Lil had been available for lunch; in fact, she'd been thrilled to hear from Ellery and insisted on treating her. Her friend's familiar bubbly warmth was a balm to Ellery's damaged dignity. The parting jab Larenz had given her regarding her clothes had added insult to grievous injury. Miserably, she wondered why he'd invited her along at all if he was going to avoid or ignore her both day and night.

'Ellery!' Small, curvy and red-headed, Lil Peters hurried across the skyscraper's forecourt and enveloped Ellery in a tight perfumed hug. 'I'm so happy to see you!'

'Me too,' Ellery replied after Lil had released her and she'd got her breath back. 'It's been too long.'

'And whose fault is that?' Lil asked, wagging a finger in front of Ellery's face before she linked arms and half-dragged her down the pavement. 'I booked us a table nearby. I don't want to wait in some wretched queue—we've got loads to say to each other, I'm sure. And I need a drink.'

Ellery smiled as she let her friend barrel her along. 'I do, as well,' she said. 'Let's order a bottle.'

Ten minutes later, they were comfortably seated in a French bistro, a bottle of Chardonnay opened between them and two glasses already poured.

'So what brings you to London?' Lil asked as she took a healthy sip of her drink. 'I thought our girls' weekend wasn't until next week.' She arched her eyebrows. 'Please tell me it's because you've finally sold Go-Mad Manor and are coming back to London to live a proper life.'

Ellery grinned. 'Not yet, I'm afraid.'

'Ellery, what are you waiting for? I understand family loyalty, of course I do, but that place is falling down around your ears.'

'Actually, I think it's reached my shoulders.' Ellery smiled and Lil just shook her head. They'd had this conversation too many times already. 'I can't sell it yet, Lil. I don't know why.' She pressed her lips together. 'I know I have to sell it eventually, but I'm not ready yet.'

Lil shook her head. 'Your father really did a number on you, Ell. It's been five years since he died, you know.'

'I know.' Her throat was tight, the two words forced out. She looked away.

'I know learning about…well, I know it was a shock,' Lil said gently. 'But surely you can let it go? You need to.'

'I've let it go,' Ellery said flatly. She tried for a smile, a lighter tone. 'It's just the house I'm holding on to.'

Lil smiled back, although Ellery knew her friend was neither satisfied nor convinced. 'So what are you doing here, then? And please don't tell me it's to buy something dreadfully boring, like curtains for your drawing room.'

'No, nothing so tedious, although I could use new curtains.' Ellery glanced down at her glass, a few bubbles bursting against its sides. 'Actually, I'm here with someone. A… man.'

'A *man*?' Lil squawked and several patrons shot her amused and curious glances.

Ellery flushed, rolling her eyes. 'Lil—'

'It's just I'm so pleased.' Lil leaned over the table, her eyes alight. 'Tell me about him. Is he the local squire in Suffolk? Or a *farmer*? I always thought they were dead sexy when they did that programme about bachelor farmers—'

'Neither.' Ellery held up a hand to stop her friend's gushing monologue. 'Actually, he is—was—a guest.'

'A guest? How romantic. Who is he? I want all the details.'

Lil's eyes widened comically. 'He's not the one you mentioned this weekend, is he? The high-maintenance one?'

'Actually, yes. But he's not as high-maintenance as I thought.' She paused. She didn't really want to mention Larenz by name; he was, she knew, somewhat famous. 'Just a man. A gorgeous man, actually.'

'Gorgeous? Really? Oh, Ellery, I'm so happy for you.' She reached over to squeeze her hand.

'It's not going anywhere,' Ellery said quickly. 'I mean it. It's just for fun. A...fling.' The word sounded awkward, coming from her. Lil, of all people, knew how few flings she'd had: zero. And how cautious she'd been with men.

'A fling,' Lil repeated thoughtfully, then gave a little shrug of acceptance. 'Sounds fabulous. And he brought you to London for a dirty weekend?'

Ellery flushed once more. 'A dirty week, actually,' she managed and took a sip of wine. 'After this, we're going to Milan.'

'*Milan!*' Once again, a few patrons glanced Lil's way but she didn't even notice. 'Just who is this man, Ellery?'

Looking at her friend's excited, animated face, Ellery knew she couldn't keep the truth from her, and she didn't even want to. Lil was her closest friend; she'd come to her father's funeral, she'd been there when her world had fallen apart.

*And it might be about to fall apart again.*

The thought slid into her mind slyly and Ellery forced it away. *No.* She was not going to get hurt, because she was in control. She was having a fling, a silly fling, and that was all. 'His name is Larenz de Luca.'

Lil's mouth dropped open so theatrically that Ellery found herself chuckling. The waiter had brought them two huge bowls of steaming pasta and she reached for her fork. 'Close your mouth. And don't shout his name from the rooftops, please. We're trying to be...discreet.'

'*Larenz de Luca,*' Lil hissed, the name still managing to carry to several tables. 'Ellery, he's just about the most eligible bachelor in Europe!'

'Is he?' Ellery felt a ripple of unease. She hadn't realized Larenz had quite that much notoriety. And yet he'd chosen *her.* 'How come I hadn't heard of him, then?'

'You don't read the gossip mags like I do,' Lil replied as she dug into her own pasta. 'And, all right, perhaps he's not the *most* eligible bachelor—there has got to be a minor prince or two that fits that title, but honestly—Larenz de Luca! He's always in the tabloids, you know, usually with some bimbo on his arm—*oh*!' She bit her lip, her blue eyes wide and contrite. 'I did *not* mean you. You know that.'

'Of course not.' Ellery's smile wavered only the tiniest bit. Lil wasn't telling her anything she hadn't known already. She'd suspected Larenz was a playboy, a womanizer; she'd gone into this with her eyes wide open. She *had.* 'I suppose he's deviating from his usual this time round, eh?'

'I suppose.' Although Lil smiled back, her eyes were still clouded with anxiety. 'I don't want you to get hurt, Ellery.'

'I'm not going to,' Ellery replied firmly. 'I told you, Lil, this is a fling. I don't want a relationship.' She smiled, reaching for her wine glass. 'Don't you know me well enough to know that?'

'Ye-es,' Lil admitted slowly, 'but I also know when you *do* fall, you'll fall hard.'

Ellery's expression hardened. 'I'm not going to fall.' Fall in love. She had no intention of doing that. No intention of stumbling into it either. Love was off-limits, for both her and Larenz.

'Why on earth was he staying at that Manor of yours?' Lil asked. 'I mean, I would have expected him to want a bit more luxury. No offence, of course—'

Now Ellery laughed with genuine amusement, the sound

a relief. 'None taken, I'm sure. I'd be the first one to admit Maddock Manor is not the pinnacle of luxury. We can't even say we have hot water any more.'

'Oh, dear.'

Ellery shrugged. 'He was there with his PR person, scouting out a photo shoot.'

'A photo shoot? At your house?' Lil looked intrigued, and Ellery laughed again.

'I know, it sounds ridiculous, doesn't it? But apparently it has some ambience.'

'And have you agreed? To the shoot?'

Ellery paused. She had neither agreed nor disagreed; the subject hadn't come up again, and she wasn't sure she wanted it to. If she agreed, she'd surely see Larenz after this week was over. That wasn't part of their agreement; it wasn't one of their terms. And yet…was it something she wanted? He wanted? 'I don't know,' she said slowly. 'Perhaps. The money would certainly help.'

'Ellery…' Lil reached over, her hand on Ellery's arm. Ellery looked up, saw the concern and compassion in her friend's eyes. 'Are you sure you know what you're doing? Larenz de Luca is…well, he's not exactly a safe bet. You know?'

'Yes,' Ellery replied lightly, 'I know.'

Lil frowned. 'Are you sure this is just a fling?'

Ellery arched her eyebrows. 'Lil, this is Larenz de Luca we're talking about.'

'No,' Lil said, 'I'm talking about you. I'm damned sure Larenz de Luca only wants a fling. But what about you, Ellery? Are you sure that's what you want?'

'Yes,' Ellery said quickly. Too quickly. And not firmly enough. For, as she gazed into her friend's face, she was suddenly struck with the alarming—and frankly terrifying— possibility that it wasn't what she wanted at all. That she wasn't in control.

That she'd been lying to herself all along.

'If you're sure,' Lil said doubtfully, and Ellery nodded.

'I'm sure.' Yet already her mind played over the conversation from last night, the way she'd been seeking Larenz out, trying to understand him, *know* him. That was not agreeing to the terms. It was not the way to keep from getting hurt. The only way to protect her heart, Ellery knew, was not to have it involved at all. And surely with a man like Larenz—a known womanizer—it shouldn't be too hard.

Except for the times when he didn't seem like the man the world knew, the playboy of the gossip magazines. When he asked her questions, when he made her lunch, when he washed her hair...

Ellery closed her eyes. She couldn't think about *that* man. She couldn't take that risk. She certainly couldn't change the terms.

She opened her eyes and gave her friend a rather hard smile. 'Don't worry, Lil. I know what I'm doing. This really is just a fling.'

At six o'clock that evening Ellery made her way into the hotel bar, her new stilettos clicking across the parquet floor. She'd bought a dress to match the shoes, a slinky number in spangled grey silk that clung to every dip and curve and shimmered when she moved. The stilettos gave her another three and a half inches at least. She'd left her hair long and loose and she'd stopped by the make-up counter at Selfridges— she'd avoided De Luca's—for a free makeover. When she'd only bought a lipstick the saleswoman had looked rather put out, but Ellery wasn't using the de Luca account. She'd pay her own way, at least for this.

She saw Larenz waiting at the bar, his back to her, his hand clenched around a tumbler of whisky. He looked tense, she thought, and stressed. Had it been a bad day at work? She didn't care. She wouldn't ask.

She knew the rules. Larenz didn't want her to ask about his day; he wanted her in bed. And she wanted him in bed. That was all they had, all they could ever have. All they wanted.

Ellery had been reminding herself of it all afternoon. Last night she'd let herself care; she'd even let herself be hurt. And that was not going to happen again.

Tonight she was going to be just what Larenz wanted—his lover. Only his lover. Not his love.

'Hello, there.' Her voice came out in a husky murmur that she'd never used before. She dropped her beaded clutch on the bar and slid onto the stool next to Larenz.

He turned, his eyes widening and then narrowing as he took in her appearance, from her tousled hair to her red pouty lips, to the dress that hugged her body, finally ending on her feet, one stiletto now dangling from one newly pedicured toe.

His mouth tightened. 'Nice shoes.'

Ellery beckoned to the bartender with one finger—she'd had her nails done too—and let her lips curve in a provocative smile. 'Why, thank you.'

'I didn't really take you for having a thing about shoes,' Larenz said. He took a long swig of his drink. The bartender came over and Ellery ordered the first cocktail she could think of—a screwdriver. Larenz's eyebrows rose but he made no comment.

'Well,' she said, jiggling her foot so her stiletto dangled a bit more, 'there are a lot of things you don't know about me.'

'So it would appear.' He glanced at her again, looking even more displeased with her appearance. Ellery felt a stab of frustration; what did he *want*? She was showing him she understood just what kind of relationship—for lack of a better word—he expected, and it still didn't satisfy him. She wondered if she ever could.

'So what did you get up to today?' Larenz finally asked, and she gave a little shrug.

'Lunch, shopping.'

'You made good use of my accounts, I see.' He didn't sound particularly annoyed but, even so, Ellery didn't feel like pointing out that she'd spent her own money. Suddenly it didn't matter. Larenz was making her feel as ridiculous as a little girl playing at dressing-up. Her cocktail arrived and Ellery took a sip. She just kept herself from making a face; she didn't normally drink hard alcohol and it tasted bitter.

Larenz shook his head slowly. 'Why are you doing this, Ellery?'

'Doing what?'

He gestured to her outfit. 'Dressing like this. Acting like this. Like a…a femme fatale!'

'Really, Larenz,' Ellery murmured, 'you give me too much credit.' She let out a husky little laugh that had several men's heads turning.

'Stop it,' Larenz bit out. 'Stop pretending. I don't know what you're trying to prove to me, but it isn't working. It isn't,' he finished coldly, 'enticing. At all.' Then, without another word, he got up from his stool and left the bar.

Ellery sat there alone, her made-up face flushing with humiliation. She felt curious and even pitying stares and, taking a deep shuddering breath, she straightened her shoulders, lifted her drink and said to nobody in particular, 'Cheers.'

Then she took a long swallow before erupting into a fit of coughing as the vodka burned down her throat.

Up in the suite, Larenz paced the room as desperate and angry as a caged panther. He didn't even know why he was so angry, why seeing Ellery like that sent him into such a rage.

The dress and make-up—hell, even the shoes—had all been high quality, well made. She'd looked sophisticated, sexy.

*Coy.* Like all the other women he'd taken to his bed. And, Larenz realized with a savage lurch of despair, he didn't want to put Ellery in that category.

Ellery was different. *He* was different when he was with her. And when she'd sashayed into the bar and spoken to him in that husky, honeyed voice he'd felt as if she'd cheapened what was between them, made it no more than a…a *fling*.

Yet it was a fling. He'd made it clear; they had a week together and that was all. He didn't *do* relationships, he wasn't looking for love.

If Ellery had been sending him a message, he should have been relieved to receive it.

Not furious.

Not *hurt.*

Fury rushed through him––fury at himself for allowing himself to care. To feel. He was breaking more rules, the most important rule of all.

Never let your heart become involved.

Ellery let herself into the suite quietly, glad at least that Larenz had given her a key that morning. She had no idea what to expect. The living room was dark, as was the bedroom. Had Larenz gone? she wondered. Checked out? Had she driven him away for good?

Perhaps it was better that way, Ellery thought wearily. She kicked off her heels, careless of them now. She didn't have a thing for shoes. She didn't have a thing for dresses or make-up or any of this. She realized she'd been pretending, playing a part because she'd thought—mistakenly, stupidly—that it was what Larenz wanted. That it was what *she* wanted.

She'd dressed like this, acted like this to convince herself more than Larenz that she understood the terms. The rules.

Yet now, disheartened and weary, she didn't care any more. It was all too confusing, too complicated. Even if he made her body sing, her heart was miserable.

She wanted to go home. Except she wasn't even sure where that was any more.

She flicked on the light in the bedroom, glancing out of the doors to the terrace as she did so. She stiffened, for a lone figure stood by the railing, hands clenched, head bowed.

Larenz.

Without considering what she was doing or why, Ellery opened the doors and stepped out into the cool night.

# CHAPTER NINE

LARENZ must have heard the door open but he didn't turn. He didn't even move.

Ellery surveyed him for a moment, surprised by the calm that had stolen over her, replacing her earlier resignation. She didn't care any more so it no longer mattered what she said. This was the secret, she thought. This was what she'd wanted all along. Not to care. If you didn't care, you couldn't get hurt. She drew a breath. 'If you wanted to make a scene, that was one way to do it.'

'I'm sorry.'

She shrugged, even though Larenz hadn't turned and couldn't s
ee her. 'I didn't realize buying a dress would annoy you quite so much.'

'And shoes.'

She thought she heard a thin thread of amusement in his voice and she chose to match his tone. 'Oh, was it the shoes? I wondered if the heels were too high.' She came to join him by the railing, gazing out at the Georgian buildings of Belgravia with a sense of cool detachment.

'I'm sorry, Ellery.' His head still lowered, Larenz turned to look at her. 'I acted like an ass.'

Ellery let out a sigh. She supposed she'd wanted an apology but, now that she had it, it didn't seem to matter or mean very much. 'I'm sorry too, I suppose,' she said after a moment. 'I don't get what it is you're trying to tell me, Larenz. I'm not…good at this.'

'What do you mean?'

'Only that I've never had this kind of no-strings affair before.' Of course he knew that; he knew she'd been a virgin. Still, Ellery tried to explain. 'I agreed to this week because, like you, I'm not interested in a relationship. I'm happy alone.' The words sounded hollow but Ellery continued anyway. 'I just don't understand how flings—'

'Don't use that word.'

'Flings?' She shrugged. 'Fine. Whatever this is…between us…I don't understand how it works. What I'm supposed to do.'

'I just want you to be yourself,' Larenz said in a low voice.

'And yet when I was myself, you stayed in the living room all night,' Ellery replied a bit sharply. 'I think I know enough to realize that when you take your lover to London, you don't sleep on the sofa.'

Larenz let out a long weary sigh and rubbed a hand over his face. 'No,' he said quietly, 'you don't.'

'So what's going on, Larenz?' Ellery asked quietly. 'Why did you get so angry? I thought I was playing by the rules.'

'Forget the rules.' Larenz cut her off, his voice nearing a savage roar. 'Forget the damn rules. Why do there have to be rules?' He turned to her and, in the sickly yellow lights from the buildings around them, Ellery thought she saw a trace of desperation in his eyes. He pulled her to him, the movement abrupt and almost rough. 'There are no rules between you and me,' he said against her mouth, and then he kissed her.

Ellery was too startled by the kiss to respond at first, and her mouth stayed slack under his as his words echoed through her. *There are no rules between you and me.*

Before she could consider that snarled statement or what

it meant, her body had kicked into gear and she responded to the kiss in instinct and need, her arms coming around Larenz's shoulders, pulling him closer to her.

Larenz kissed her like a drowning man, and her touch was his only anchor. In all the times he'd kissed her, she'd never felt so needed. So necessary. And so she kissed him, imbuing it with all the hope she felt, hope that now buoyed up within her even though, moments ago, she'd been as near despair as Larenz seemed to be.

He swept her into his arms in one easy movement and Ellery couldn't help but laugh. 'You know, you do the Rhett Butler thing very well,' she murmured. 'I haven't been carried so much in my life.'

'Sometimes grand gestures are needed,' Larenz replied and took her into the bedroom.

After that, there was little need for words.

Ellery must have dozed after they'd made love, for when she awoke, slowly, blinking in the darkness, she saw it was near ten o'clock at night. Too late for the dining room but, as her stomach gave a rumble, she realized she was starving.

Next to her, Larenz stirred—he must have slept, too—and lifted his head to glance at the clock. When he saw the time he groaned and fell back on the pillows.

'I take it we missed our dinner reservation?' Ellery teased, and he smiled and reached for the telephone on the bedside table.

'Room service it is, then.'

They ate in bed, feeding each other bits of this or that, for Larenz had seemed to order at least a dozen dishes.

'We'll get crumbs all over the sheets,' Ellery protested, laughing, and Larenz just gave her a wicked smile.

'I can think of worse things. Besides, I don't intend for us to do much sleeping.'

Yet eventually—nearing dawn—they did sleep, Ellery's

head on his shoulder, his arm wrapped protectively around her. As she tumbled slowly into sleep, Ellery found herself wondering how everything had changed—for it surely had—and how, when only hours before, things had felt so confused and unhappy and *wrong*, they could now feel so wonderfully right.

Her eyes fluttered closed and she refused to think about it any more. For surely that could only lead to doubt, and then to fear.

No, she would trust whatever had happened, whatever had changed, and she would enjoy this precious new bond with Larenz…for however long it lasted.

The next morning Ellery awoke in Larenz's arms as he dropped a kiss on her head and said, 'Wake up, *dormigliona*. We need to catch an eleven o'clock flight to Milan.'

'What?' Ellery struggled towards consciousness; several nights in a row of only a few hours' sleep—if that—had left her feeling groggy and disorientated.

Larenz, she saw a bit resentfully, pushing her tangled hair behind her ears, looked fresh and energised.

'I have a business meeting late this afternoon,' he told her as he headed towards the en suite bathroom. 'And then a party this evening for the launch of Marina. I want you to wear one of its signature gowns.'

'You do?' Ellery drew her knees up to her chest, her mind spinning and her heart thudding at the sudden turn of events.

'Yes, so get dressed!' He popped his head out of the bathroom door. 'The shower is big enough for two, you know.'

Two hours later, they were sitting comfortably in first class as the jet rose into a dank grey sky, breaking though the clouds to dazzling blue. It was an apt metaphor for her own life, Ellery reflected as she gazed out of the window, for she felt as if the clouds and cobwebs enshrouding her own mind and heart had been swept clean away. For now. She slid a glance at Larenz, who was reading the paper. He looked, Ellery thought, rather adorably serious, yet he must have felt her eyes upon him for, after a few seconds, he glanced up, smiled and reached for her hand.

They remained holding hands as Ellery settled into her seat and watched the last of the clouds disappear below them, no more than forgotten wispy shreds.

Once in Milan, Larenz ushered Ellery into a waiting limo; within minutes they were speeding away from Milan's Linate Airport towards the city centre.

'I have a suite at the Principe di Savoia,' Larenz told her. 'I'll need to go straight to the office but I've booked a set of spa treatments for you this afternoon.' He touched her hand briefly. 'I want you to feel completely pampered.'

'I already do,' Ellery murmured. Larenz smiled and squeezed her hand.

The limo pulled up in front of the impressive white facade of the Hotel Principe di Savoia, one of Milan's oldest and most luxurious hotels. And Larenz, Ellery soon found out, had the most luxurious suite.

He hadn't even got out of the limo when it pulled up to the hotel, so Ellery was escorted to the Presidential Suite on her own. She stood in the centre of the living room, turning in slow circles as she took in the panelled ceiling, the priceless art work and the windows that overlooked the suite's private swimming pool with its muralled walls and marble pillars, the dolphin mosaics giving it the look of a decadent Roman bath.

In the bedroom, her feet sank into the cushy comfort of a plush carpet that had clearly been modelled on the Aubusson design; this one, however, wasn't threadbare like Maddock Manor's.

Amazed, laughing, Ellery fell onto the king-sized bed,

revelling in the wondrous luxury, only to sit bolt upright when a knock sounded at the door of the suite.

She opened it to find a sleek-looking young woman smiling at her. 'Signorina Dunant? I am here to begin your spa treatments.'

Ellery had never had any kind of spa treatment; the entire notion was alien to her and conjured vague images of something halfway between pleasure and pain. She soon found out she'd been quite wrong.

Stretched out by the Pompeiian-style pool, she had an hour-long massage that nearly put her to sleep, followed by a set of facials and waxings and mineral therapies that left her feeling as shiny and sleek as one of the dolphins depicted in the mosaic. Every inch of her glowed or even sparkled.

She felt utterly rejuvenated, both inside and out.

A staff member had brought her lunch; another one had provided the finest selection of magazines. The young woman, Maria, who had first greeted her, tucked her into bed several hours later, informing her that she would return to dress her in two hours.

Ellery fell promptly asleep.

She woke to another knock at the door and, before she could even call out, Maria slipped into the room, a gown swathed in plastic draped over one arm.

'*Buona sera, signorina*,' she called out cheerfully. Then, in English, 'I come to dress you.'

Ellery slipped out of bed and watched as Maria first took out the most delicate, exquisite undergarments she had ever seen. 'These first.'

Ellery obeyed, exchanging the robe she'd slept in for the fragile lace. They felt like gossamer on her body, like silken cobwebs. She tried to glance in the mirror but Maria, smiling, shook her head and wagged a finger at her.

'Not yet. Wait until the whole ensemble, it is finished.

Now the dress.' She undid the plastic to reveal the most beautiful and breathtaking dress Ellery had ever seen.

Made of shimmering lavender silk, it fell in a waterfall of colour from a simple strapless design, ending in a discreet yet dazzling row of lighter violet ruffles. It was a fairy-tale dress, a Cinderella dress, a dress in which to feel like a pampered princess. And Ellery couldn't wait to wear it.

Maria helped her into it, advising her to sit carefully so as not to crush the gorgeous material. She styled her hair into a loose chignon, allowing a few artful tendrils to frame Ellery's face. And then came the make-up: Ellery had never worn so much, yet, when she finally looked in the mirror, she didn't look overly painted, just a better and more beautiful version of herself.

She looked, Ellery thought as she took in her own appearance, amazing. The dress hugged her bust and waist before swirling around her; Ellery turned in a quick, dizzying circle and laughed as the dress flew out around her.

'Signor de Luca sent these,' Maria said, holding up a magnificent pair of diamond teardrop earrings. They were real, Ellery knew, and had to be worth around half a million pounds. She fastened them in her ears with shaking fingers. 'And these,' Maria added. 'He selected them in particular, apparently.'

Ellery opened the box to stare, smiling, down at the pair of diamond-studded stiletto sandals. Although they would hardly be seen under the gown, they still complemented the outfit perfectly and were the most amazing shoes she'd ever seen. She put them on and Maria handed her the final touch: a gauzy wrap in pale violet. Ellery slid it over her shoulders.

'Signor de Luca will meet you in the hotel lobby.'

Ellery gave a shaky little laugh. She could hardly believe that any of this was real, that she—like this—was real. A few days ago she'd been scrubbing the kitchen floor, and now she was Cinderella about to go to the ball. And, at some point, whether tonight or tomorrow or five days from now, like Cinderella, she would most certainly lose all these gorgeous trappings. This had to end. Yet she didn't want to think that way. She didn't want to ruin the most magical night of her life with worries or fears. She just wanted to enjoy. To revel. She smiled at Maria. 'Thank you for all of this.'

As she came out of the lift into the hotel's opulent lobby, she saw Larenz right away. How could anyone fail to notice him, she wondered, for he was by far the most breathtaking man in the room. His curly hair had been tamed and combed back from his face and his powerful frame was perfection in an exquisitely fitting tuxedo. He turned when she left the lift, as if he'd sensed her presence, and then all of time and life itself seemed suspended as her eyes met his and held his gaze for an endless, enchanting moment.

Larenz took in her hair, her gown, her feet in one single sweep of his eyes that left Ellery breathless when she saw the blatant admiration and appreciation glinting in their navy depths.

He strode towards her, curling one arm around her waist to bring her into contact with the hard wall of his chest. Ellery lifted her face for a kiss but he brushed a kiss across her forehead instead. '*Magnifica*. I don't want to spoil your make-up.'

'Don't worry—'

'That gown matches your eyes perfectly. We should call that colour "Ellery".'

'You can't—'

Larenz arched an eyebrow. 'No? Perhaps a little more mystery is required. Do you know, when I first saw you I remarked on your eyes? I thought they were the colour of a bruise, but that is far too sad. They are happy now,' he whispered in her ear, 'the colour of the most beautiful sunset I have ever seen.'

Ellery let out a little bubble of laughter. 'Is this the famous Italian charm?'

'You've only noticed now?' Larenz pretended to sound hurt. 'Come, our car is waiting.' He bent his head to murmur in her ear, 'And, as always, nice shoes.'

The party was held in another of Milan's best hotels but, so dazzled by everything, Ellery could barely take in the glinting chandeliers, black-suited waiters circulating with champagne, the clink of crystal and melodious tinkle of a piano offset by the low steady murmur of a hundred different conversations. Yet they all stilled to silence when she entered the ballroom on Larenz's arm.

Ellery felt herself freeze as five hundred pairs of eyes seemed to train right on her. 'They are wondering who this Cinderella is,' Larenz murmured. 'And, of course, the men are jealous of me.'

'And the women?' she tried to joke.

'Wish they were so beautiful,' Larenz replied smoothly, 'of course.'

Yet the unreality of the evening didn't fade as Ellery circulated through the ballroom, glued to Larenz's side, watching as he chatted and laughed easily—mainly in Italian—with hundreds of different people.

After two hours Ellery had a headache from the constant noise, and a raging thirst from having consumed nothing but two glasses of champagne since they'd arrived. Her beautiful dress felt a little tight under her arms and her shoes pinched her toes. Besides that, all she'd had to eat since noon was a salad and she was starving.

Standing next to Larenz as he joked in Italian with a balding businessman, she had an intense, insane desire to be tucked up in bed with a bowl of popcorn and a good book.

'Dinner is about to be served,' Larenz told her. 'You have been so patient, enduring all these business conversations.'

Ellery tried to smile. 'It's nothing.'

'Still, I'm sure you're hungry.'

'Yes... I'll just nip to the loo first. I'd like to freshen up before we sit down.'

She made her way through the maze of people, grateful for the blast of cooler air when she finally emerged from the crowded, overheated ballroom. A waiter directed her to the ladies' room, which was blissfully empty. She had just gone into a stall when she heard two women enter, speaking for once in English.

'Have you seen de Luca's latest?' one woman asked, her voice sounding bored and laconic.

'That wilting flower? She won't last long.'

Ellery froze, then leaned forward to glimpse the two women now reapplying their lipstick in front of the huge gilt mirror.

'They never last long with Larenz,' the first woman observed. 'Yet he seems to be giving this one the star treatment. That gown is from his new line of fashion, and did you see those earrings? She looks like such a little mouse. Larenz must have given them to her.'

The second woman let out a trill of sharp laughter. 'Payment for services rendered. She must not be such a mouse in bed.' She smacked her lips and capped the tube of lipstick. 'He always gives them the star treatment before the axe falls.'

'Well, this one should be gone by tomorrow, then. I thought he was seeing someone else—a Greek girl, Al-something.'

'That heiress? No, he sent her packing ages ago.' The woman shrugged and capped her lipstick. 'Oh, well. I'm sure we've just about seen the last of this mistress. I wonder who he'll be on to next.'

Ellery didn't hear the rest of the conversation; the buzzing in her ears was too loud. She waited until they had gone and the room was empty again before she left the stall. In the mirror, her face looked pale and shocked.

The gossip hadn't surprised her; she'd known, of course she'd known, that Larenz had had plenty of women. She'd even known they didn't last long. And whether or not *she* would last long—well, she knew just how long she was meant to last.

No, none of the casual yet vicious gossip had surprised her; it was the word the woman had used so carelessly.

*Mistress.*

She was Larenz's mistress—a woman to be used and discarded. Just like her father had used and discarded both his wife and his own mistress—the woman who had shattered both her and her mother's worlds.

These clothes, these jewels, these *shoes*—all of it was... what had the woman said? Payment for services rendered. She was a bought woman, a scarlet woman, a *slut*—

This wasn't just a fling; she had no control. These rules, these terms, were not hers. This wasn't, Ellery realized numbly, remotely what she'd wanted. She'd been such a fool, thinking it was. Convincing herself it was. And, worse, she'd been fooling herself in believing that Larenz might now feel more for her than a passing fancy—

*He always gives them the star treatment before the axe falls.*

Standing there, gasping, reeling from pain, Ellery felt it had already fallen.

# CHAPTER TEN

Somehow, Ellery made it back to the ballroom; by that time everyone was filing out towards the dining room. She couldn't see Larenz and for once she was glad. She had no idea what she would say to him.

She was horribly conscious of the curious gazes and speculative stares, and now they no longer held admiration or even jealousy but malice or pity. Everyone here—the cream of European society—knew that she was Larenz's mistress. Expected her to be on the way out of the door. Accepted that she had received this gown, these jewels, everything—for sex.

The only reason she was here was because she'd had sex with Larenz de Luca.

Of course. It was obvious; she couldn't understand how she'd not made the connection before. She'd deceived herself so unbearably, Ellery thought. A hard knot of misery lodged in her middle, spreading outwards and taking over her whole body. She'd told Larenz, told Lil, told *herself* that she'd wanted a fling. She'd believed it. At least, her mind had.

Her heart wanted something else entirely. Her heart wanted a relationship. Her heart, she realized despondently, wanted love.

And, with the word *mistress* echoing horribly in her mind,

she fully understood just how much of a fool she'd been, how empty what she had with Larenz—she couldn't even call it a relationship—was.

Blindly, she left the crowds heading into the dining room, hurrying through the lobby so fast she nearly slammed into someone and one of her stiletto sandals slipped from her foot. Ellery barely noticed until a young porter grabbed it and caught up with her.

'*Signorina! Signorina! Vostro pattino!*'

Ellery took it blindly, mumbling, '*Grazie... grazie...*'

'Just like Cinderella, eh?' The porter said in English, and Ellery flashed him an utterly mirthless smile.

'Yes, just like Cinderella,' she replied woodenly. She'd already turned into a pumpkin and it wasn't even midnight.

She took a taxi back to the Savoia. At the concierge desk, she asked for another room and the man behind the desk frowned at her.

'It is not necessary, *signorina*—'

'Yes, it is,' Ellery said firmly. 'How much is your...most basic...room?'

The man frowned again and quoted a price that Ellery could never afford. Swallowing, she said, '*Scusi*...you're right, it's not necessary.'

She needed to get her things from the Presidential Suite anyway, and she should at least write Larenz a note and explain.

Yet how could she explain? How could she articulate that she'd agreed to his damned terms, to this whole wretched fling, because she'd thought she'd be in control? She'd thought she wouldn't be like her mother then, waiting and pining and miserable. She'd thought she could handle it.

Yet, hearing those women in the ladies' room, Ellery had realized she wasn't like her mother at all. She was worse. She was like her father's mistress. That was what this fling was: accepting presents, staying in gorgeous hotels, being wined and dined and *spoiled*, just as Larenz said, and all because she was his lover. His mistress. Payment for services rendered. An agreement whose terms he had chosen.

She felt like an idiot for not making the connection before, for not realizing what it all meant. *Of course* she was Larenz's mistress. Of course a fling with a rich and powerful man would end up being like that.

Yet she'd been so determined not to act like her mother, she'd ended up acting like something far worse instead: the woman she despised, the woman who had stolen her father's heart, not only from her mother but from her, too. The woman who had taken everything from her, even her memories, leaving her only Maddock Manor.

*That* was why she stayed.

And it was why she had to leave now. She couldn't be that kind of woman. She couldn't even pretend to be that woman for a moment.

Ellery dragged herself up to the suite, fumbling with the key card, and finally managed to unlock the door, kicking off her hated sandals as she entered the living room.

'What the hell were you doing?'

Ellery froze in shock. Larenz stood in the centre of the living room and he looked furious.

'How did you get here?' she managed numbly.

'I saw you running from the party and took a taxi back here.'

'And got here before I did,' Ellery noted, still dazed. The wrap slid from her shoulders and puddled on the floor.

Larenz shrugged one shoulder. 'You don't know Milan. The driver most likely took a longer route to earn a few more euros.'

'I see,' she managed, moving into the room like a sleepwalker.

'Well, I don't,' Larenz retorted and, even in her shocked state, she heard the current of pulsing rage in his voice. 'Why did you leave the party without even telling me? Do you realize how many people saw you? Including a few journalists—it will be in all the papers tomorrow, how de Luca's mistress ran out on him!'

Ellery froze. She turned slowly to face Larenz. Even in the face of his obvious anger, she felt suddenly, eerily calm. 'That's the first time you've used that word with me.'

Larenz looked nonplussed. 'What are you talking about?'

'Mistress. You called me your mistress.'

A certain wariness replaced his anger. 'It's just a word, Ellery.'

She took a deep breath; this was something she understood. 'No, it's not, Larenz. It's an attitude.'

He let out an exasperated breath. 'Fine. Whatever. Why did you leave the party?'

Ellery just shook her head. She couldn't believe how much had changed, or how flimsy the bond between them had really been. She'd thought everything had changed last night, when Larenz had told her there were no rules. Yet there were still rules—just rules for her and not for him. 'I left because I received a much-needed wake-up call,' she finally said.

'A wake-up call? What are you talking about, Ellery?'

'I heard two women in the ladies' room,' Ellery said, her throat tightening, 'talking about *me*—'

Larenz cursed under his breath. In two strides he'd reached her and his hands clasped her bare shoulders. His skin was warm. 'Ellery, you must know it is just gossip. Malicious—'

'Oh, yes, I know that,' Ellery choked out. 'Of course I do. I may have been a naive virgin, but I'm not completely stupid.'

'Then what—'

'I'm your mistress, Larenz, aren't I? That's what this week is.' Somehow she found the strength to twist away from his grasp. She walked to the doors of the terrace and gazed out at the darkened sky. 'I came with you to London, to here, thinking it was just a fling, some fun. Thinking I could handle it. And I admit it's my own fault for being so stupid. For not seeing the forest for the trees.'

'You are not,' Larenz gritted out, 'making the least bit of sense.'

'No, I know I'm not,' Ellery agreed. Her voice sounded so reasonable, yet she knew underneath that thin veneer of calm was a boiling river of hurt and shame. 'And I freely admit that my reaction to that word—mistress—is purely emotional,' she continued in that same reasonable voice. 'Irrational, even. It doesn't change how I feel, I'm afraid.'

Larenz shrugged impatiently. 'I don't understand any of this.'

'And I finally understand everything,' Ellery returned. 'These lovely earrings—' She took off the precious earrings and dropped them onto the coffee table. 'And these—' She kicked off the sandals. 'All of it, payment for sex. Because, if I weren't sleeping with you, I wouldn't be here.'

'This is ridiculous. What are you saying, Ellery? I can't give you things? *Gifts?*'

'But they're not gifts. Our relationship—if I could even call it that—isn't equal. Because you're calling the shots, Larenz. When you tire of me, whenever that is, you'll send me packing. Discard me…like…' She bit back the words she'd been going to use: *my mother.* 'Like an old shoe.'

Larenz stilled. 'When I invited you to come with me, you knew the terms of the arrangement—'

'Oh, yes, I knew the rules. And they *do* apply, don't they? You're the only one who is allowed to break or change or even forget them for a moment.' She drew in a ragged breath. 'Yes, I knew them. But I didn't realize how they would make me feel.'

'You agreed,' Larenz said, his voice quietly icy. 'You

made it quite clear, in fact, that they suited you, too. You weren't looking for a relationship, Ellery. Or love. Or did you deceive me?'

'I deceived myself,' Ellery said flatly. 'Because I thought that's what I wanted. Or could want, at least.'

'I see.'

'No, you don't.'

All of a sudden all the self-righteous anger drained out of her, leaving her only weary and depressed. 'I knew,' she said quietly. 'And so it might not seem fair that I'm changing my mind. But I can't do this, Larenz. I can't be your—or any man's—mistress.'

'I tell you, Ellery, it is just a word!' Larenz exploded. 'Why let it upset you?'

'Because it's more than just a word to me.' Ellery smiled at him sadly. 'Perhaps I should tell you why I stay at Maddock Manor.'

Larenz regarded her warily. 'Fine.'

She drew a breath, knowing she needed to explain and yet not wanting to expose herself, not to Larenz when he was like this, so cold and angry and hard. And she'd actually been afraid—for a little while—that she might fall in love with him.

Letting out a little sigh, Ellery sank onto the sofa. Her dress—her gorgeous dress—poufed all around her. 'I told you I loved my father,' she began. She stared out of the window, not wanting to look at Larenz or attempt to read his emotions. 'He was charismatic, charming, larger than life.' She spoke dully, reeling the list off as if reading from a script. That was all it had been: the script of her father's false life.

'He was never good with money,' she told Larenz. 'He inherited everything from his father, although the property and title aren't entailed. Looking back, I suppose the Manor fell slowly into disrepair over the years, slowly enough that I never really noticed. When I was little, it was my home and

I loved it. When I got older, I was too busy with my own life to notice or perhaps even to care.'

Larenz gave a little shrug. Although he was listening, he still seemed impatient. 'It is always so with the young.'

'I suppose. Anyway, that's not the point of what I'm telling you. I just want you to understand…everything.' She looked at him then but saw his expression hadn't changed. She made herself continue. 'My father used to go away on trips. Business trips, he called them, although he didn't have a job as such. He had investments—concerns, he said.' She gave a sudden bitter laugh that had Larenz raising his eyebrows although he said nothing. 'Yes, concerns. Two of them, in particular.' She broke off, drew a breath and then looked at Larenz directly. 'He'd be gone for days, sometimes weeks at a time. My mother always told me he was doing it for us, to make sure we could stay in our lovely manor house. I think she genuinely believed that—that he was working on these investments of his. At least she made herself believe it, although, looking back, I know she suspected…something. She was certainly unhappy. But neither of us found out the whole truth until he died, when I was nineteen.'

Larenz narrowed his eyes. 'What happened then?'

'My father's secret was revealed,' Ellery said flatly. 'Both of them. He had a *mistress*, you see. A mistress and…' her voice hitched '…a son.' Larenz's mouth tightened but he said nothing. 'A son.' She shook her head, reliving the shock and horror she'd felt on that day, still numb from grief, when her father's *other* family had come to Maddock Manor and she'd realized how they had been as grief-stricken and *loved* as she and her mother. 'He visited them,' she explained dully. 'When he was gone. He had a whole other life—a whole other family. They lived in Colchester, in quite a nice house, which he provided—part of the reason why the Manor was falling into such disrepair. Funding two separate existences is quite expensive.'

She let out her breath slowly. 'We didn't believe them at first. Wouldn't someone have known? Wouldn't someone have said something? After all, tooling around Colchester in a vintage Rolls isn't exactly cloak-and-dagger.' She tried for a laugh and failed. Her fear was that people *had* known and had kept the secret out of pity. 'Anyway, the woman showed my mother photographs taken throughout the years. Birthdays, even Christmases when my father said he just had to be away. A whole life.'

Ellery had stared at those photographs with a numb sense of disbelief; she'd gazed at the pictures of her father playing football with the son he'd always wanted—and had had. Her mother's face had closed in on itself as she'd looked at several snaps of her husband kissing another woman and, worse than that, far worse than that, were the photos of the kind of family life they'd lost years ago, that her father had been enjoying all along. With someone else. It had been the worst kind of betrayal, for both of them.

'What is her name?'

Ellery glanced at him, startled. 'You mean my mother…?'

'No,' Larenz replied flatly, 'your father's mistress. What is her name? Did you know? Do you remember?'

She stared at him, nonplussed. 'Diane,' she said after a moment.

'And the son?'

Ellery didn't speak for a moment. 'David,' she finally said quietly. 'He's just a year younger than me. Why do you want to know?'

Larenz shrugged. 'No reason.' He paused, the silence tense and impatient. 'I don't see what this has to do with you or me.'

*You or me.* Not *you and me*. Perhaps there wasn't a *you and me* any more, that essential *us*. There never had been.

Ellery swallowed. 'Because I want you to understand…I

agreed to this week, Larenz, because I thought it would be different. *I* would be different. I've spent most of my adult life trying not to be like my mother, pining away for a man who wouldn't love her. It's why I avoided relationships, why I was a virgin.' She gave a tiny humourless laugh. 'And so I came on this fling because I thought it would be a way to take control. To choose for myself. To *not* be like her. And,' she added fairly, 'I wanted to. I wanted to be with you.' Larenz said nothing and Ellery finished painfully, 'But I ended up being something worse than my mother. I ended up being like my father's mistress. A mistress,' she repeated, her words filled with self-loathing. 'I can't be that.'

'But I'm not married,' Larenz said flatly. 'It's not the same.'

'No,' Ellery agreed, 'not exactly. I realize that. But it's not…we're not…equals, are we? And this whole thing—' she flung her arm out to encompass the discarded earrings, the sumptuous king-sized bed, everything '—isn't what I wanted. It isn't me.'

'What you're really saying,' Larenz said in a voice whose quietness still spoke of an underlying fury, 'is that you do want a relationship.' He spoke the word with scathing disdain. 'Love, even.'

Ellery blinked. She didn't want to admit it. She didn't want to be so vulnerable, and especially not with Larenz when he looked like this, so cold, so contemptuous. He certainly didn't want love, not from her, not from anyone. 'I don't know what I want,' she finally said in a small tight voice. 'Just not this.'

Not this, and yet she still wanted Larenz. Her body ached with the memory of his touch, and her heart ached, too. Even now, when he stared at her so coldly, unmoved by her sordid little story, she wanted to love him. To be loved. The thought was terrifying. She'd been fighting it all along, denying it to herself, yet the truth was so appallingly obvious that Ellery wondered how she'd managed to dupe herself—not to mention Larenz—for so long. Silly, stupid her.

She was a very inconvenient mistress.

'Anyway, I'm sorry for being difficult,' she finally managed, half amazed by her own apology. The feelings surely ran too deep for a simple sorry, yet she didn't know what else to say, how to bridge this chasm that had opened between them, wide and yawning. 'I know this wasn't what we agreed on.' She wondered why she'd told him at all. He *was* right; her father's past—her past—had nothing to do with Larenz and her. It was just *her* problem, her baggage, and the reason why she was standing here alone, the heart she'd sworn wouldn't get involved now breaking, just as her mother's had.

Larenz watched Ellery's slight shoulders slump, her head bowed, the pain he knew she'd been holding inside for far too long now spilling out, even though she tried to keep it back. From him.

His heart twisted, it tore, for he knew what kind of heartache she'd experienced in her father's betrayal. He understood all too well how it made you alone and afraid. Afraid to trust, to love. Staying alone was safer.

Wasn't he the same?

And yet he was, Larenz thought, all too different. What she'd told him tonight confirmed that.

Even so, he wanted to take her in his arms, to smooth the hair from her forehead and kiss the tears shimmering in her eyes—she blinked them back, bravely—and tell her the past didn't matter at all.

But of course he couldn't, because it did. The past mattered very much, and it was what kept them both here, suspended in silence, neither of them able to cross the chasm that now yawned between them.

And he was furious—*furious* that she'd reneged on their terms and broken their rules.

And furious with himself for doing the same.

'I'll go and change,' Ellery whispered, her voice breaking, and Larenz stifled a curse. He didn't want it to end like this, broken and despairing. He didn't want Ellery to leave.

He wasn't, Larenz knew, ready to let her go. Even if at some point it was inevitable. Even if letting her go now would be the smartest—and safest—thing he could do. For both of them.

'Wait.' He spoke gruffly, his throat tight. He didn't know what words to say, what would help. What would be enough and yet not too much for, God knew, he didn't know even now what he was capable of feeling. Giving. 'Let me help you,' he finally said.

She turned, surprised, wary and perhaps a little hopeful. Larenz forced his face into a smile. He didn't know what he wanted. He didn't know what he wanted to *feel*.

'Let's not end it like this, Ellery.'

Her mouth turned down at the corners, drooping, and so did her eyes. 'I'm not sure I really see the point of going on.'

'There are…' Larenz paused, his throat drying, tightening, and he forced the words out '…there are things I have to tell you, too.' He could hardly believe he was saying the words. Ellery may have trusted him with her secrets, but he had no intention of revealing his.

Did he?

Why did this woman make him want to share his tightly held self, reveal the parts of himself he kept hidden from the world?

He felt as if he were teetering on the edge of that chasm between them and he couldn't bridge it. He could only jump.

'You do?' Ellery asked softly, and Larenz jerked his head in the semblance of a nod. He felt far too close to breaking, to falling. And he had no idea if he would tumble into the abyss below, or if trust—and love—would help him to fly. It was a frightening feeling, this uncertainty, this defencelesness. He didn't like it.

'Later,' he said almost roughly. 'There will be time for it later.' And Larenz didn't know whether that was a threat or a promise…or simply a hope.

She nodded slowly, accepting and, reaching for her hand, Larenz led her into the bedroom. He didn't trust himself to speak; he had no more words.

When Ellery awoke the next morning her body ached as if she'd been climbing a mountain. She felt as if she had and the summit was nowhere in sight. As she lay there, the morning sunlight bathing her face, she wondered just how long she'd been climbing; it surely wasn't a matter of a single day.

So much of the last few years had been caught up in that ceaseless striving, trying to make sense of her life when her father's revelations had scattered all the truths she'd built her very self on.

*This is my family. This is who I am. I am loved.*

She rolled over to look at Larenz; he was still sleeping. She wasn't sure what had happened last night, if somehow she and Larenz had found a way forward. They hadn't spoken much after she'd told him about her family. Words were too dangerous, the bond between them too fragile. Ellery had gone to bed alone, only to wake up in the middle of the night to find Larenz sleeping next to her, as he was now.

She gazed at his face, the lines and angles softened in sleep, his lashes touching his cheeks. She wondered what thoughts hid in his head, what hopes in his heart. She wondered if she would ever have the courage to ask, or if he would have the courage to tell her.

She wondered what was going to happen next. Now.

Then, quite suddenly, his eyes opened and Ellery was caught staring.

'Good morning,' Larenz said, his voice husky with sleep. 'You're looking at me as if I'm a puzzle and you're trying to work me out.'

She knew she could never do that, or at least not yet. She didn't have all the pieces. 'Nothing so dramatic,' Ellery said, keeping her voice light. 'I just like watching you sleep.'

Larenz caught her hand and pressed it to his lips, his eyes on hers. Ellery's heart turned over at the gesture, and what it could possibly mean. She didn't dare ask. She simply accepted it for what it was rather than what it might be. 'I want to show you some of my life,' he said.

His life. His *self*. Hope fluttered inside her. 'I want to see it,' she said, her hand still caught in his. 'Where are you taking me?'

'De Luca's and then, perhaps, Umbria. Where I'm from.'

And Ellery knew this was his way of giving her something, perhaps of bridging the chasm that had opened between them—the chasm between a fling and a relationship.

They drove in a chauffered limo to De Luca's flagship store in the centre of Milan. Housed in an art nouveau building, it was five storeys of sumptuous elegance. The crowds parted like the Red Sea for Larenz and staff flocked to his side, eager to do his bidding. Ellery simply marvelled at it all: the soaring marble pillars, the fabulous jewellery and linens and clothes, the feeling that she'd been catapulted into a film or a dream.

He showed her everything; he knew everything. Every worker's name, every piece of merchandise. He owned the store, not just in the literal sense but in a spiritual way, as well. It was utterly his.

'How do you know so much?' Ellery asked as they rode

the old-fashioned lift upstairs, complete with brass grille and uniformed attendant.

Larenz gave a little shrug. 'It's my job to know everything.' He paused. 'I started as an errand boy for the head of a department store. Marchand's, it was called. I watched everything there and I saw all the waste and corruption and greed. And I knew—even then—that I wanted to start something better, bigger. Something that celebrated the beautiful without making you feel ugly.' He gave a little self-conscious laugh, a sound like nothing else Ellery had ever heard from him, and she knew this was another gift. He was showing her himself.

Over the course of the afternoon he took her to every department at De Luca's, and not once did he offer to buy her anything. Ellery knew it was intentional, knew he was keeping her from feeling like a dreaded mistress. Funny, how this lack of gifts could feel like a gift in and of itself; how much she appreciated the true gift Larenz was giving her: his time, his self.

And it was, she knew, making her fall in love with him. Love. The forbidden word, the word she could only whisper to herself because it made her so afraid. Love was scary. Risky. Love was a big, dangerous unknown.

And she couldn't think about it for too long.

At the end of the day they returned to the hotel, weary, foot-sore, happy. Larenz ordered food in and they ate in the soft glow of candlelight in the sitting room. They didn't speak much, as if they both knew that words could break this precious, fragile bond that had emerged between them, tenuous and tender.

When Larenz simply reached for her hand and led her to the bedroom, Ellery went. She didn't ask questions, not of Larenz, not of herself. She simply did. She simply was.

They made love silently, slowly, and it felt like the purest form of communication. The joining of bodies, of minds, of *hearts.* As Larenz entered her, his eyes fixed on hers, Ellery felt tears start to come. She blinked them back, unnerved, undone because, even now, she hadn't expected *this*.

She hadn't expected Larenz to reach her, to find her, and yet he had. As she lay in his arms afterwards she didn't let herself wonder, question, regret. She simply lay there, listening to the sound of their breathing; even their lungs found an innate mutual rhythm. And she let herself be at peace.

The next morning they drove out of Milan in Larenz's silver Porsche, the sky high and blue above them. After an hour or so of driving, Larenz turned off the motorway and took a narrow road through the rolling hills of Umbria, now russet and ochre with autumn, bathed in sunlight.

'Just where are we going, exactly?' Ellery asked. They hadn't spoken much in the car. Words were still dangerous, fraught with possibility. Silence, Ellery reflected, was truly golden.

'A palazzo near Spoleto,' Larenz replied. 'My home, of sorts.'

After another hour of driving, he finally turned up a long tree-shaded drive; at its end Ellery could see a magnificent palazzo, two dozen windows glittering in the sunlight.

So this was where Larenz grew up, she thought as he parked the car and turned off the ignition. A child of power and privilege. His shoes crunched on the gravel as he came around to open her door.

'Does anyone live here now?' Ellery asked as she followed Larenz to the palazzo's main entrance. There was a strangely empty feel to the place; the windows looked blank and, although everything was excellently maintained, it felt sterile and barren. Lifeless.

'No.' Larenz took a key from his pocket and opened the door. Ellery heard the rapid beeping of a security alarm before he shut it off. 'Come in,' he said with a wry, rather twisted smile, 'to my Maddock Manor.'

Ellery stepped into a soaring hall, the floor tiled in gleaming black-and-white chequered marble. Above her a huge crystal chandelier glinted in the sunlight streaming from the diamond-paned window above the front door. She gave a little laugh. 'This is nothing like Maddock Manor.'

'I suppose I was speaking figuratively,' Larenz replied. He tossed the key on a marble-topped table by the door and turned around in a slow circle. 'Do you know, I've never been in here before.'

'What?' Ellery turned to face him, her mouth slackening in shock. 'What do you mean? Isn't this your home?' Yet, even as she said the words, she acknowledged that Larenz didn't have a home. He lived in hotels—temporary, impersonal, luxurious. Now she wondered if there was a reason for that…and if he was going to tell her now.

'This is my father's home,' Larenz corrected. 'He died three years ago, which was when I bought it.' His mouth twisted in something like a smile, although the expression still chilled Ellery. It held so much darkness, so much pain. 'Our fathers, you see, were very similar.'

'Larenz…how…' Ellery trailed off uncertainly, for there was something forbidding about his expression, something bitter in his voice. She didn't know what to say, what questions to ask. He was giving her another gift, another part of himself, and she was afraid to receive it.

'Come on,' he said in that same bitter, brittle voice. 'We might as well see what my money has bought.' He strode off towards one of the reception rooms and, after a moment, uncertainly, Ellery followed.

Larenz walked up and down the drawing room, inspecting the priceless antiques and artwork with a critical eye. Ellery stood in the doorway and gazed around the room; everything was burnished, polished and in perfect condition. The air smelled faintly of lemon polish and it looked as if a maid had just left the room.

Yet Larenz had never lived here? *No one* lived here?

It was, Ellery decided, strange. Unsettling.

'Larenz? What's going on? Why have you never lived here?'

He stood in front of what looked like an original Gaugin and studied it for a moment. 'Not bad, I suppose.'

'Larenz—'

'I never lived here because I was never allowed,' he said, cutting her off, his voice sounding curiously unemotional. 'This was my father's home…and he did not recognize me as his son.'

Ellery's breath came out in a rush. 'What do you—'

'You see, we're from opposite sides of the blanket, Ellery,' Larenz said with a strange little smile. 'Yet the same sordid story.' Ellery just shook her head, not understanding, yet knowing somehow that what Larenz was telling her was terribly, horribly important. 'My mother,' he clarified, 'was my father's *mistress*.' His delicate emphasis on the word made Ellery flinch.

*It's just a word.*

Was this the reason he believed that? Was this the reason he never let anyone close? She felt blood rush to her face as she thought of all the bitter, damning things she'd said about her own father's mistress, and that mistress's *son*.

A man like Larenz. Luckier than Larenz, for at least her father's son had been acknowledged. Loved. Larenz, Ellery knew then with icy clarity, had not.

'And what happened?' she whispered.

Larenz shrugged. 'My mother worked in the kitchen here. Classic story, you know?' He gave a little laugh, almost as if it bored him. Yet Ellery heard—and felt—the hurt underneath and knew his father's rejection had wounded him the same way hers had. He'd felt the same fierce betrayal, felt it now, and the thought filled her with a deep, sudden sorrow. 'She got pregnant, she was let go, my father gave her a little money.' His mouth twisted. 'He didn't set her up in a nice little house in Colchester, that was for certain.' His voice caught, tore. 'He didn't spend birthdays or Christmases with his other little family. No holiday snaps, I'm afraid.'

Ellery blinked back tears. They gathered at the corners of her eyes, threatening to spill. She'd been so callous, lost in her own sad little story without a single thought for Larenz's. If only she'd known. If only she'd asked. 'Did she love him?' Ellery asked quietly. She wanted to ask—*did you*? Had Larenz—in his own different way—been as disappointed by his father as she had been by hers? Or perhaps even more? He'd received nothing from his father. At least she had memories, tarnished as they were.

Larenz shrugged. 'Who knows? She doesn't talk about it very much. She was ashamed—an unmarried pregnant woman in rural Italy a generation ago was a very hard thing to be.' He walked over to the window, leaning one shoulder against its frame as he stared out at the gardens, manicured to the point of sterility. 'That was why she moved to Naples—her sister was there and she wanted to get away from the gossip.'

'And what about you? Did you ever meet your father?'

Larenz tensed; at least Ellery thought he tensed, although he didn't seem to move. She felt it in the air, suddenly taut with suppressed emotion. 'Once.' The single word did not invite more questions, yet Ellery longed to ask. To know.

'And this house?' Ellery asked for a moment. 'How did you come to own it?'

'Now that's an interesting question.' Larenz turned away from the window. 'Why don't we go ahead and see the rest of it?'

Wordlessly, Ellery followed Larenz out of the drawing room. He headed up the curving marble stairs and then down a hallway lined with wood-panelled doors. Their steps were silent on the sumptuous carpet. He barely glanced in the bedrooms, each one decorated, as far as Ellery could tell from her hurried glances, with the utmost elegance and luxury.

If this was his Maddock Manor, she thought rather ruefully, it looked a lot better than hers.

Back downstairs, he paused in a library, the walls lined in leather-spined books. He trailed one finger along the titles, a look of dispassionate calm on his face. It made her ache, for she knew how that blank expression could hide so much feeling. She'd felt it on her own face, and the turbulent, boiling emotions underneath, as well. 'Larenz—' she began, but he just shook his head. He didn't want to talk. He was shutting her out with his silence, and she couldn't bear it. She wouldn't let him.

'So?' she finally asked, her voice sharp. 'Does it live up to your expectations?'

Larenz dropped his hand from the shelves. 'No,' he said after a moment. 'I don't know what I expected to feel the first time I walked across that threshold, but...' He shook his head slowly. 'I don't really feel anything.' He gave a sad little laugh. 'Stupid, eh? Pathetic. I bought this house when my father died as a way to show I was worthy of it. At least I suppose that's why, if I'm going to indulge in a little psychoanalysis.' He let out a long weary sigh. 'Just like your father, mine was terrible with money. By the time he died, I was able to pick this place up for a song. And his family, of course, was furious.' Ellery heard the way he scornfully emphasised *family* and felt the sting of tears once more.

She realized that in all of her maudlin musings on her father's double life, she'd never considered how his other family felt; how hard it must have been to feel like the impostors, hidden away, unable to claim him as their own. She'd felt betrayed, yet they must have, as well.

And so must Larenz, whose own father had never even

acknowledged him. Had his father's rejection made him the man he was, Ellery wondered bleakly, unwilling and perhaps even unable to love, or even to have a relationship longer than a few weeks? And, if that was the case, how could she reach him? How could they ever find a way forward—if there was even one to begin with?

They were so different, yet so unbearably alike, crippled by their families' failures, holding on to the one tangible thing that proved they'd had families at all: *houses*. And, while Larenz's palazzo was in immaculate condition, it was as much a millstone to him as Maddock Manor was to her.

'Larenz—' She took a step forward, hope lurching inside her, making her almost stumble. She would not give way to despair; she'd done that for too long, and so had Larenz. At least they were alike. They were the same at least in this, and knowing that made her realize this impossible chasm could, in fact, be bridged. What had seemed to keep them apart could, possibly, *hopefully*, draw them together.

If they were willing to take the risk. If she was.

'What is it?' Lost in his own thoughts, he turned to her as if he'd forgotten she was even there. He looked blank, bored, and she knew he was closing himself off again.

And then Ellery understood what she needed to do—and what Larenz needed to do. She closed the space between them and reached up to touch his shoulders, letting her hands slide along the silk of his suit, drawing him to her. He tensed, resisting, and she let her own body relax into his, daring him to accept her own surrender. She wouldn't let this separate them. She wouldn't let either of them back off, shut down. Stay safe. 'Take me to your real home,' Ellery said. 'In Naples. Is your mother still there?'

'Yes—'

'Take me there,' Ellery implored quietly, her body still nestled into his. 'Show me your home, not this…this mausoleum. Show me *you*.'

Larenz shook his head, the movement one of instinctive denial and self-protection. 'I've never taken anyone there.'

'Take me.' Ellery held her breath, knowing how much she was asking. Her heart bumped against her chest, against Larenz's, and the silence stretched on. 'Please,' she whispered and, tilting her face up so she could see his, she saw expression after expression chase each other across Larenz's features. Denial, fear, uncertainty, hope. She knew them all herself. Felt them deeply, these painful feelings that could in fact—maybe, *please*—bind them together. After an endless moment Larenz finally answered.

He put his arms around her, drawing her even closer into the shelter of his own body, and buried his face in the warm curve of her neck, his lips grazing her skin. This was, she knew, his own surrender. 'All right,' he whispered, and Ellery closed her eyes in relief and gratitude as the sun's rays slanted through the long elegant windows of the palazzo and bathed them in warmth and light.

# CHAPTER ELEVEN

DARKNESS was falling by the time they reached Naples. It had been a long day driving, for Naples was at least four hundred miles from Milan, and yet, for all the time they'd spent in the car, Larenz and Ellery had hardly spoken. The memories were too thick, too suffocating, and yet, even in the midst of them Ellery felt a small strong ray of hope. She'd felt it in Larenz's arms and she clung to it now, even through the silence, the growing tension. The memories were strong but she wouldn't let them win. She would not be defeated.

Larenz glanced at Ellery, her profile pale against the darkened window. She looked tired and a little sad, and he could hardly blame her. The last few days had been a hell of a roller coaster; he felt their toll in every part of his body, especially his heart.

He'd never wanted this. To care—and, perhaps, God help him, even more than that. He couldn't voice it. He wasn't sure he could even feel it, and he wasn't about to tell Ellery any of it, and yet the thought of her leaving…

Larenz's fingers tightened on the steering wheel. Taking Ellery to Naples—to his past—was surely a way to guarantee that she *would* leave. He might exhibit the trappings of wealth and privilege now, but he certainly didn't come from it. Even his mother, ever proud, refused his offer of a house in the better part of town. She still lived in the cramped flat he'd grown up in, much to Larenz's dismay and even disgust.

And perhaps Ellery's, as well… Most women, he'd found, weren't interested in anything but the man he'd become. Not the man he'd been. Not even the man he was. Yet, from nearly the moment he'd met Ellery, he'd been revealing the man he truly was, as if he *wanted* to be known.

It was maddening. Frightening. Why—and how—did she make him reveal his secrets, make him long for that dangerous vulnerability? What would she really think of the boy whose father had told him he didn't know him, who had turned him away from his door—the same door Larenz had opened that morning? Possessing the palazzo was an empty victory; the man he'd been trying to impress was already dead. Yet Larenz hadn't realized that—fully understood the futility of his grand gesture—until he'd shown the place to Ellery. Until he'd seen the grand empty rooms through her eyes.

Sighing, Larenz steered the Porsche through the narrow streets of one of the city's solidly working-class neighbourhoods. This was his childhood, his home, and he felt its shabbiness keenly. Ellery gazed at the apartment buildings with their peeling paint and shutters askew, her face impassive.

It wasn't much different than her Manor, Larenz supposed, although there weren't any Aubussons here, threadbare or otherwise. He nudged the Porsche into a street parking spot, a few inches on either side of the bumpers. 'Here we are.' His voice sounded tight and strained even to his own ears.

'Will your car…' Ellery asked hesitantly.

Larenz pressed the lock on his key, smiling grimly. 'No one would dare touch my car here,' he said. 'They know me. And they know my mother.' He saw her flicker of surprise and wondered how she would react to his mother's cramped flat, her oppressively working-class background, her refusal to accept the world Larenz now inhabited. Would Ellery feel as stifled by that life—that love—as he did?

He'd rung his mother from the road to say he was coming home; she'd crowed with delight and promised plenty of pasta. Now, leading Ellery down a narrow alley to one of the buildings in the back, he wondered if he was making the biggest—and most heart-wrenching—mistake of his life.

This wasn't what she'd expected. Perhaps she should have expected it, Ellery acknowledged, although, considering Larenz's own wealth, she hardly thought his mother would still live in a crumbling apartment building in what was certainly not one of the finer neighbourhoods of Naples. Judging by the tight set of his jaw, Ellery wondered if Larenz wished his mother lived in more comfortable circumstances. Had she refused his money? For a proud man like Larenz, who must have worked his way up to his current stunning level of success, that must have been hard to accept.

She was beginning to understand why he hadn't taken anyone here, why he'd been reluctant to take her. She was beginning to understand so much of this man she'd once judged as simply entitled and shallow. He was, she knew now, anything but.

'*Buon sera! Buon sera!*' The door in front of them had been thrown open, and a woman in her fifties, her curly greying hair pulled back from her smiling face, stood there. She grabbed Larenz by the shoulders and kissed him soundly on both cheeks. Ellery didn't understand the sudden stream of Italian the woman fired at her son but, from the wagging finger and teasing frown, she suspected Larenz's mother was telling him he didn't visit or eat enough. From their embrace, she knew their relationship had to be warm, yet she could still feel the undercurrent of something—tension? resentment?— tautening the air.

'Mamma, this is Ellery Dunant, Lady—'

'Nice to meet you,' Ellery interjected hurriedly. Why on earth would Larenz use her stupid title now? Was he *trying* to emphasize their differences? She wanted to focus on the similarities. 'Please, call me Ellery.'

'And I am Marina de Luca. It is a pleasure,' Larenz's mother said in halting English. Ellery gave Larenz an involuntary startled glance when she heard his mother's name. Marina. He'd named his line of haute couture after his mother. The realization made her heart twist.

Marina shooed them both inside. 'Come in, I've kept dinner.'

'Of course,' Larenz murmured to Ellery and she smiled. It was good to see Larenz out of his element, and yet also in it. Good and unsettling, too, because he most certainly wasn't the man she'd once thought he was, the man he wanted the world to believe he was.

In the past few days he'd been—willingly, even—showing her someone else. The man he really was. And that man, Ellery knew, was someone she could love.

She swallowed, pushing the thought away. It was too much—too frightening—to deal with now, even though the thought kept creeping up on her mind, twining its way around her heart.

She gazed around the small tidy living room with its framed embroidery, the sofa and chair covered in crocheted slipcovers. The room was cosy in a worn way; it was a million miles from Larenz's luxuriously sterile hotel suites. It was his home.

Marina took a huge dish of rigatoni out of the oven in the tiny kitchen and brought it to the small table in the dining nook. 'Here. Eat. You must be hungry.'

'This looks delicious,' Ellery murmured as she sat down. 'I'm sorry I don't know any Italian, but your English is very good.'

Marina beamed. 'Larenz, he teach me,' she said.

'Really?' She shot a quick speculative glance towards Larenz, but he simply shrugged. He seemed uncomfortable here, almost embarrassed. Ellery knew he didn't like showing her this part of himself, his true self, and she wanted to show him it was okay. She accepted it; she accepted him.

'Eat,' Marina said again and, knowing that food could be love, Ellery did. It was indeed delicious.

Afterwards Marina plied them with tiny cups of espresso and meltingly scrumptious slices of *panetta*.

'Larenz, he never brings anyone to see me,' she said as she watched Ellery eat her cake. 'I sometimes think he is ashamed.'

'Mamma, you know that's not true,' Larenz said quietly. His own cake was untouched.

She shrugged pragmatically. 'I know how far you've come in this world. I can understand how this is a step down for you.'

'It's not,' Larenz said in a low voice. Ellery's heart ached at the intensity she heard.

Marina turned to Ellery. 'Larenz, he wanted me to live in a big place on the outskirts of town. A palazzo! Can you imagine? What would the neighbours say? Who would visit me then?'

Even though Ellery understood the older woman's predicament, she felt a shaft of sympathetic sorrow for Larenz. He'd tried to provide for his mother, and she wouldn't take his money, his love.

Marina glanced at her son, bemused and affectionate. 'Besides Larenz. And he only comes a few times a year, if that.'

'I'm sure Larenz is very busy,' Ellery said quietly, smiling at him, but he only looked away and Marina let out a laugh.

'Oh, yes,' she agreed, 'very busy. But no one should be too busy, eh?'

'I need to make a few calls,' Larenz said and excused himself from the dining area.

A silence stretched between the two women. Ellery couldn't tell if it was friendly or not. Marina gazed at her in an assessing way as Ellery toyed with her fork. Her mind buzzed with all the new things she'd learned today, all the parts of Larenz that he'd shown her. Now she had to process them. Accept them. 'This was all so delicious,' Ellery finally said. 'Thank you.'

'He's never brought a woman to see me,' Marina said quietly. 'You know? A woman...friend.'

Ellery glanced up, blushing. 'Oh. Yes.'

'But you. He brings you.' She shook her head slowly. 'English girl. I don't know...'

'It's not...' Ellery began, having no idea what to say or how to explain. She didn't know what her relationship to Larenz was; the uncertainty was overwhelming, on both sides. She wanted more—at least, part of her did—but even now she was afraid. Everything had happened so quickly, so intensely, and she didn't know whether to trust it. Trust Larenz, trust herself.

Marina leaned forward, her eyes narrowed. 'You don't break his heart, eh? I know he has money, but inside? He is just a poor city boy. That's all he ever was, and he can never forget it.' She sat back, sighing. 'I know how many mistakes I've made,' she said quietly.

'I don't want to break anyone's heart,' Ellery said, her throat turning tight. She didn't add, *and I don't want mine broken either*. They didn't speak again until Larenz came back in the room.

'I reserved us a room at a hotel in town,' he said. He reached down to kiss his mother's cheek. 'It's late, Mamma, and we drove all day from Milan. But tomorrow we'll come back. Perhaps we can take a walk in the city gardens?'

'Why would I want to walk?' Marina said a bit grumpily. 'You know how it makes my feet ache.'

'What about those new trainers I bought you? They're supposed to help.'

Marina shrugged, and Larenz gave a tiny sigh. 'They weren't that expensive,' he said quietly, and she just shrugged again.

Outside, they didn't speak as Larenz unlocked the car and opened Ellery's door before sliding into the driver's seat.

'Thank you for taking me,' Ellery finally said, and he shrugged.

'Now you know.'

*Know what?* Ellery wondered as Larenz pulled away from the kerb and headed towards the historic district of the city. Know where he came from? Know what he'd experienced and endured? Know that even though he had money, and power, and prestige, he still was that poor city boy underneath, and she loved that about him?

*Loved.*

Ellery swallowed. *Now you know.* Yet, despite all this, despite how full her heart and mind both were, she still felt as if she didn't know anything. Every thought, every assumption and belief she had was shaken, overthrown, leaving her with nothing more than a handful of doubts. And hope, too, tiny and precious.

They drove in silence to the Hotel Excelsior, yet another luxury hotel, this one on the Bay of Naples. As Ellery took in the stunning architecture, the opulent lobby and, of course, the magnificent penthouse suite, she realized she felt only tired. This wasn't her; this wasn't even Larenz. It was just a way—a luxurious way—to keep from really living.

She had so many unnamed hopes, yet she could not give voice to them, even to herself. She was too afraid. Too much had happened too quickly. She couldn't trust if it was real,

if it even existed at all. She sank onto the bed and closed
her eyes.

Yet why did the thought of leaving him make her want to
cry?

'Don't cry, *cara*,' he said softly. Ellery felt the feather-
light touch of his finger on her cheek and opened her eyes.

Larenz knelt in front of her, his face full of such a sorrowful compassion that another tear slipped down her cheek.
She hadn't even realized the first one had fallen. She let out
a little choked sound, halfway between a laugh and a sob. 'I
don't know why I'm crying.'

'It's strange, is it not?' Larenz said. He brushed the second
tear from her cheek. 'So much has happened in so little time.
It is hard to know what to think.'

Ellery swallowed. *Or what to feel.* Yet, as they sat there in
the half-darkness of the room, the only sound their unsettled
breathing, she was reminded of that night at Maddock Manor
when he'd held her so close, when he'd let her decide.

When they'd made love. And, perhaps, when she'd fallen
in love.

For surely she loved him? Surely this was love, this restless churning, this fierce hope, this deep need? She rested
her forehead against his and let the realization—the hope and
the need—trickle slowly, certainly, through her.

She loved him. Perhaps since she'd first seen him walking
so arrogantly into her home and resented him for it; certainly
later, when she'd seen the little thoughtfulnesses that betrayed
the man he truly was. A man with humble beginnings, who
still cared for his mother. A man who washed her hair and
wiped away her tears. A man as afraid of love and the hurt
it could cause as she was.

Or perhaps more.

Yet still she loved him. The thought was wonderful.
Terrifying. For she had no idea if he loved her back, and
she was afraid—so afraid—to find out. Afraid to test the

weight of the bridge Larenz had built across this chasm between them.

Ellery drew a shuddering breath. She drew back just a little. In the shadowy room she couldn't quite see Larenz's expression. She wanted to say something of what she felt but the words clogged in her throat. Fear kept them in.

Larenz lifted a hand to touch her cheek again. A shaft of moonlight bathed his face in silver, illuminating his expression of hungry hope, almost like desperation. 'Ellery—'

His mobile phone buzzed like an angry insect in his breast pocket and, with a muttered curse, Larenz reached to turn it off.

And then Ellery spoke, not from the love rising inside her but from the fear that was determined to keep it down. 'No, you should answer it. It might be your mother—'

Larenz gave her a strange look, his lips thinning, and then he glanced at the little glowing screen of his phone. 'It's just a business call,' he said flatly.

Ellery rose from the bed. She barely knew what she was saying, only that she was so afraid to make this jump, to let herself feel. Love.

Be hurt.

'Then you should certainly get it,' she said, her voice sounding absurdly false and light. 'It's bound to be important.'

'You want me to answer it?' Larenz said, and he sounded incredulous.

Ellery forced the single word through numb lips. 'Yes.'

'Damn it, Ellery—' His voice turned raw, ragged, and Ellery nearly broke inside. Yet the numbness and fear still held and she shook her head.

'Answer it, Larenz.' She knew she was telling him much more than to answer a call, and it made her heart break. She was pushing him away and she didn't know how to stop.

With another muttered curse, he punched a button on his phone and spoke tersely into it.

Ellery left the room.

Larenz snapped the phone shut and tossed it on the bedside table. A stupid business call, and it had ruined what had been one of the most important moments of his life. Almost.

He felt rage course through him and, worse, far worse than that, hurt.

He was hurt. He was a blind, stupid fool, for he'd let someone get close enough to hurt him and he *never* did that, not since the day he'd walked up that endless drive to his father's palazzo and raised the heavy brass knocker. Not since his father had, reluctantly, seen him, his eyes shrewd, his face cold.

*I'm Marina de Luca's son*, Larenz had said. He'd been fourteen, tall and bony and awkward, not yet a man. *I've been wanting to meet you.*

*I don't know you.*

He'd tripped over his words in his haste to explain, to reassure. *I don't want anything from you. I know...how it is. I just wanted to see you...* The longing in his voice! Larenz closed his eyes now as he remembered. There had not been a shred of pity or compassion in his father's face. Yet there had been knowledge. Larenz had seen that. His father had recognized him, or at least had known who he was.

*I don't know you. Goodbye.*

He'd closed the door in Larenz's face. A moment later, one of the staff had escorted him from the property, making it quite clear that Larenz was never to return again, unless he wanted trouble.

From that moment on, Larenz had hardened his heart. He'd done it methodically, deliberately, knowing full well what he was doing and why. He'd never let anyone get close, never cared when he was mocked or teased, as he had been for that one hellish year at Eton. His mother had told him he'd won a scholarship; it was only later he'd learned that his father, in a moment of guilt, had funded his sorry education.

Larenz had walked out the moment he'd learned. He wouldn't take a penny from anyone, and certainly not from the man who'd sired him.

From then on he'd kept acquaintances, employees, mistresses. Not friends, not lovers. No one came close. No one touched him, no one made him need or even want.

Except Ellery.

Somehow Ellery had slipped past his defences without even knowing she was doing so. She'd touched him with her bruised eyes and fierce pride and sweet abandon in his arms. He'd begun to believe it could all *mean* something.

And in that treacherous moment he'd been about to say— what? That he *loved* her? Larenz didn't know what words had been about to come out of his mouth, from deep in his heart, but they would have meant something to him. Too much.

And she'd told him to answer a damn call.

Larenz glanced at his discarded mobile. He felt his head clear, his heart harden once more. It felt good. Right. Safe. This was who he was—who he'd made himself be. Who he had to be. He let out a long slow breath. He'd just come very, very close to making a terrible mistake.

Thank God he hadn't made it.


In the living room, Ellery sat on the sofa and stared sightlessly out of the window. Her mind was spinning, seeking answers to questions her heart was demanding. Why had she made Larenz take that call? Why hadn't she let him speak?

Had she been afraid he was going to tell her that he didn't love her…or that he did?

Which was more terrifying?

Love was so scary, Ellery thought with a distant numbness. Opening yourself up to all kinds of pain. And with a man like Larenz...

*He's not that kind of man. That's just your excuse, because you're so damn frightened.*

She let out a shuddering sigh that was far too close to a sob. Larenz came into the room and she felt his silence, heavy and oppressive with unspoken words. She couldn't bear it. She had to say something, anything. 'I've had quite the whirlwind tour of Italy,' she made herself say, her voice cringingly bright. 'I haven't been here since my sixth-form year, on a school trip—'

'Ellery.' She stopped, alarmed by his tone. It was flat and final and unlike anything she'd ever heard from him before. 'It's over.'

Ellery opened her mouth soundlessly and then closed it again. Her mind spun in empty circles. She couldn't think of a single thing to say, so she just repeated his own word. 'Over?'

'Yes.' Larenz didn't look at her as he crossed to the suite's minibar and poured himself a whisky. 'I have to get back to work. I'll put you on a flight back to London in the morning.'

Ellery blinked. She supposed she should have expected something like this and yet, considering what had just happened...what she'd been afraid was going to happen...

What she'd *wanted* to happen.

She swallowed, her mouth turning terribly dry. 'Just like that?'

He shrugged, his back to her. 'You knew the rules, remember?' The words sounded like a sneer.

'And you told me there were no rules between you and me,' Ellery flung back, her voice breaking, the sound of vulnerability, of need. This was what she hadn't wanted, this hurt and pain, but now that it was here, coursing through her, she found a new kind of courage, the kind borne of desperation.

She drew a breath. 'Larenz, I know I acted…strangely…a few moments ago, when I told you to answer the phone, but I was scared… This is all so new to me… I've never felt…' She was babbling, unaware of what she was saying, the words coming from the well of need and fear—a far greater fear—that a life without Larenz in it was far worse than the pain of rejection.

'It's over.' Larenz's voice was low, savage. 'Don't embarrass yourself, please.'

*Embarrass* herself? Was that what she was doing? Ellery blinked hard, as though she'd been slapped; her head reeled as if she'd been hit. Hurt. Suddenly she wondered if, in her own desperation and desire, she'd completely misread the situation. Maybe that conversation really *had* been about a phone call.

Maybe Larenz was used to these intense, crazy weeklong affairs, maybe this was how he always acted with his *mistresses*.

She'd fallen for his damn *lines*.

And then another line came to her: *She hath no loyal knight and true, the Lady of Shalott.*

There was too much damn truth in that wretched poem, Ellery thought bitterly. Too much truth, and she was tired of it. She wouldn't be Larenz's failure; she didn't buy the unhappy ending or the sentimental tragedy. She felt cold, and clear, and quietly angry. She rose, standing before him; his back was still turned. 'Fine,' she said, and her voice sounded as flat and final as his. 'Since it's over, you can sleep on the sofa.'

She'd made it to the bedroom door before Larenz spoke again. 'By the way, that was my assistant calling to tell me Amelie wants to start the photo shoot next week. The normal fee is ten thousand pounds. I'll send you a cheque.'

Ellery stiffened. Her hand shook as she reached for the doorknob. 'Fine,' she said, and went into the bedroom.

# CHAPTER TWELVE

ELLERY must have slept, for she awoke in the morning, gritty-eyed, her body aching, her heart like lead inside her. Sunlight poured through the windows and in the distance the Bay of Naples sparkled like a diamond-scattered mirror.

The world was moving on.

She swung her legs over the side of the bed and sat there for a moment, her head bowed, her hair hanging down. She let herself feel the agony of rejection, the intense pain of loss, and then she pushed it all down, deep down inside.

She was moving on, too.

Dressed in a pair of jeans and a woollen jumper—Maddock clothes—she came into the living room with her bag packed, her manner brisk.

Larenz was already showered and dressed, a mobile clamped to his ear. His sweeping gaze took in her clothes, her bag, her purposeful expression, and then he turned away.

Ellery poured herself a cup of coffee from the cafetière left on a tray and took two bitter sips. Larenz shut his phone. 'I called you a taxi.'

Ellery put her cup down. She felt worse than a mistress; she felt like a whore. 'Thanks, but it's not necessary. I can find my own transport.'

An emotion flickered across Larenz's face, darkening his

eyes, but Ellery couldn't tell what it was. She made herself not care.

'I booked you a flight to London, first class. You change in Milan.'

'Again,' Ellery replied, her voice crisp, 'it's not necessary.'

Now she recognized the expression on Larenz's face: impatience. 'Ellery, you don't need to make a point. You can't afford a plane ticket—'

'Actually, I can—' Ellery cut him off coolly '—considering I'm ten thousand pounds richer.'

'And shouldn't that money go towards the house?' Larenz demanded, and Ellery faced him with blazing eyes.

'I hardly think,' she told him coldly, 'that you're in any position to offer me advice.'

Larenz exhaled impatiently, and Ellery reached for her bag. The fact that her heart was breaking and he just looked tired and impatient made her feel both furious and pathetic. He was done. Well, so was she.

'Goodbye, Larenz,' she said coolly, without looking at him, and then she walked out of the door.

Larenz stood in the centre of the suite, the sound of a door closing echoing through his empty heart. Except it wasn't empty any more; it was far too full.

He'd cut off Ellery to keep himself from getting hurt and it hadn't worked. He ached all over, inside and out. He was crippled with pain.

And that, he told himself savagely, was surely a sign that he'd made the right decision. Even if it was agonising.

Ellery booked the cheapest flight to London, which required three changes and took twenty-four hours. By the time she stumbled out of Heathrow, she was exhausted and yet she had another journey to make.

She took a train to Bodmin and then hired a taxi for the journey to her mother's cottage near Padstow. Anne Dunant rented a modest place on the outskirts of the town where she worked as a librarian. In the six months since her mother had left Maddock Manor, Ellery had only been there once. Now she took in the neatly tended garden, the welcome mat in front of the door, the vase of flowers in the window and was glad her mother had made a life for herself, away from the Manor. Away from the memories.

Her mother opened the door before she could knock and enveloped Ellery in a quick, fierce hug before she uttered a word. 'I'm so glad you came.'

'Me too,' Ellery said. It had been a sudden and surprising decision during the long hours of her endless flight from Naples, but one she'd realized she needed to take before she got on with her life.

'Come in, I've made tea.'

'Thanks. I'm exhausted.'

'I'm sure you are. What on earth were you doing in Italy?' Her mother, still elegant at fifty, and in jeans and a jumper, moved into the cottage's tiny kitchen. It was all such a far cry from the space and elegance of Maddock Manor—at least in its glory days—but Ellery knew that wasn't a bad thing.

It wasn't a bad thing at all.

'I was on holiday of sorts,' she said after a moment. 'With a man.'

Anne paused, the kettle in her hand. 'Promising?' she asked and Ellery smiled wearily.

'No.'

'I'm sorry.' She made the tea and brought it over to the sitting room that led directly off the kitchen. 'I worry about you, you know, stuck up in Suffolk all alone.' Her mother gave her a rather shaky smile. 'I know you wanted to keep that place, Ellery, and I understand, but—'

'It's all right.' Ellery smiled back and took a sip of tea.

'I wanted to thank you for letting me stay there, actually. I realize if you'd sold it you could have been a lot more comfortable—'

Anne waved a hand in dismissal. 'Ellery, I'm fine. And how could I sell the only home you knew? It's your inheritance. It's not mine to give away.'

Ellery nodded, her mug cradled between her hands. 'Still. Thank you. I realize...' Her throat suddenly ached and she took another sip of tea. 'I realize I needed to live there for a while. I needed to...think about things. And,' she added, swallowing past the tightness, 'I needed to get away. Get some perspective.'

'And did you?' Anne asked quietly.

'Yes.' Ellery nodded and put her mug down. 'Yes, I did. It wasn't easy or comfortable, but I did. In fact, I have some ideas I wanted to talk to you about.'

Anne smiled and reached for Ellery's hand. 'I can't wait to hear them.'

Growing up, Ellery had loved her father more than her mother; he had taken up all the space in her heart with his booming laugh and bear hugs, his absences making her, predictably, love him all the more. Her mother had been remote, removed, lost, no doubt, in her own secret heartache. Yet, in the five years since his death, they'd slowly and steadily drawn closer, brought together by her father's betrayal, by their own disappointments and now, Ellery hoped, by their determination and desire to build new and better lives.

The past was done. She was moving on.

As the taxi turned up the Manor's sweeping drive, Ellery's jaw dropped in soundless shock. The lawns were covered with camera crews and their endless equipment, and a trailer had been parked on the gravel in front of the house.

'Something going on, luv?' the driver asked as he pulled up. Ellery took a few pound coins from her purse.

'I suppose so,' she said and got out of the car.

She'd spent the weekend at her mother's cottage, a relaxed respite from her current cares, and yet clearly life had gone on, plans had been made and put into action without her approval or even her permission.

As the taxi disappeared down the drive, Ellery saw Amelie come around the corner of the house, swathed in faux fur, a mobile clamped to her ear. When she caught sight of her, she snapped the phone shut, her mouth curving into a horribly false smile.

'*Sweetie!* We've been wondering when you'd get back.'

'I was in Cornwall, visiting my mother,' Ellery said tightly. 'What on earth is going on?'

'The photo shoot, of course.' Amelie tucked her arm into Ellery's; she'd never been so close to the woman before, and her perfume overpowered even the crisp scent of leaves and frost in the air. 'We need to have the photos out by Christmas.'

'What if I hadn't come back?' Ellery couldn't help but ask. Amelie's arrogance was unbelievable.

'Oh, I knew you would,' Amelie replied cosily as she steered Ellery towards her own front door. 'After all, where would you go?'

There was no malice in the question, and Ellery felt too tired to bother mustering a sense of affront.

'So could you open the house?' Amelie asked, depositing Ellery on the portico. 'We've been doing the outside shots but we need to get inside.'

'Amelie, I just got back. This is a bit inconvenient—'

'Trust me, sweetie, ten thousand pounds is worth a little inconvenience.'

Ellery shook her head in disbelief. Even now, Amelie was acting as if she owned the place, as if a bit of money made that much difference. Yet she couldn't seem to get angry; she was too weary and careworn.

So she smiled instead as she unlocked the door. 'I suppose you're right. That money will make a huge difference.'

'Won't it just,' Amelie agreed and breezed past her into the hall. Ellery said nothing. She wasn't about to tell Amelie Weyton about her plans.

She spent the next two days holed up in her bedroom, spending the time on her laptop and mobile, arranging her affairs. Occasionally she'd go downstairs for something to eat and see the models' make-up being done in the kitchen; if she wandered to the window, she saw shots being posed from a distance. The models looked artfully lethargic, their beautiful faces blankly bored.

It wasn't until the last day of the shoot that she realized just why Larenz had decided on Maddock Manor. She'd stayed out of the rooms they were using for actual photography yet, curious for once, she peeped into the drawing room to see a model splayed in front of the fireplace—*their* fireplace—and her jaw dropped. Her heart ached.

The room had been transformed, and terribly. Fake cobwebs hung from the chandelier and bookcases, and everything had been coated with some kind of imitation dust or grime. The curtains at the windows, while shabby, had been in decent condition; they were now replaced with utter tatters.

It looked, Ellery realized, like the mouldering wreck Amelie had claimed it was. It looked like a ghost house, a ruin, a *hovel*. She felt a tight burning in her chest.

'Isn't it amazing?'

Ellery spun around to see Amelie smiling happily at her. 'They did *such* a good job with the cobwebs. We hired a film-set designer. Look how the gown stands out,' she murmured, turning Ellery back around again. Ellery gazed at the blank-faced girl in a gorgeous fuchsia gown splayed against the now grimy marble. Yes, the colour did stand out against all the gloom and dust; Ellery was level-headed enough to see that there was indeed something artistic about the shot. Beauty and the Beast.

But this was her house. Her *home*. The place she'd been trying to keep afloat for the past six months, and this photo shoot felt like a mockery of everything she'd made of it, everything she'd been.

And Larenz had known all along.

She took in a deep breath and let it out again. She was moving on, past the house, past the hurt. She thought of the money and where it was going and she turned to Amelie with a cool smile. 'Yes,' she agreed, 'very artistic. Today's the last day?'

Amelie had the audacity to pat her cheek. 'We'll be out of here before teatime, sweetie. That's a promise.'

And they were. Ellery watched as they packed up their cameras and vans, the models climbing almost sulkily into a waiting limo. They'd removed all the trappings of decay, and Amelie had even arranged for a professional cleaning service to come and restore the rooms they'd used to their former glory. If there had been any mocking irony in her voice, Ellery hadn't heard it.

Amelie was, apparently, among other things, a professional.

Ellery turned from the window and went to the kitchen to make herself a much-needed cup of tea. The house felt very empty now, and she was glad she would be leaving again soon.

'Hello, Ellery.'

Ellery whirled from the sink where she'd been filling the kettle. Larenz stood in the kitchen doorway; a gust of cold air blew in from the open door and rattled the windowpanes.

'What are you doing here?' Ellery managed. She couldn't think of anything else to say, for she was too busy drinking him in greedily, her eyes lingering on his crisp curling hair, his glinting eyes, the hint of stubble on his jaw. He wore a woollen trenchcoat and held a pair of leather gloves in one hand. His cheeks were reddened with cold.

'May I come in?'

Ellery realized she'd left the tap running and turned it off. 'Yes. I suppose… Why are you here, Larenz?'

'I came to give you the cheque.'

'Oh.' It was ridiculous to feel disappointed. For a moment—seeing him again—her spirits had buoyed, sailing far too high as her heart forgot every hurtful thing he'd done and said.

Now she remembered.

She grabbed the kettle and plonked it on the stove. 'You could have posted it, you know.'

'I didn't want it to go astray. It's a lot of money.'

'Not to you.'

'Just because I have a lot of money,' Larenz said, 'doesn't mean I don't value it.'

'Oh, well, at least that's something you value.' Ellery closed her eyes, her back still to Larenz. She sounded far too spiteful and hurt, and she didn't want to be. She *wasn't*. She was moving on, forgetting Larenz, forgetting the foolish hopes she'd once had, so briefly—

'Ellery—'

'Thanks, anyway.' She turned around quickly and held out her hand.

Larenz didn't move. His gaze held hers, intense and even urgent, yet he didn't say anything and neither did she.

'I'm sorry,' he finally said quietly, 'for the way things happened.'

It was so little. So damned little. He made it sound as if it had been an accident, a twist of fate or nature, rather than his coldblooded decision to end things in such a callous way, to treat her as no more than the mistress she'd always been.

Ellery smiled coolly. 'The cheque, please, Larenz.'

'Ellery—'

'Why did you come here?' she demanded, her voice only a little raw. 'What did you hope to gain? There's nothing between us, Larenz. There never was. You made that quite clear when you dismissed me from your presence—'

'It wasn't—'

'Oh, but it was. And coming back here and seeing this photo shoot you authorised? Turning my home into some kind of mouldering mockery—Amelie explained it all—'

Larenz flinched. 'It's just a photo shoot, Ellery, and I knew the money—'

'Damn the money! And damn all your *justs*. It's not just a photo shoot, or just a word, or just a fling. Not to me.' Her voice shook and she strove to level it. 'I suppose that's how you keep your distance, how you justify it all to yourself. Everything—everyone—is *just*. No one comes close enough to be more than that.'

'Don't,' Larenz said quietly, but the word still sounded dangerous, a threat.

'I won't,' Ellery replied simply. 'I'm done. I thought, for a little while, that I loved you. Or at least that I *could* love you, which was quite a big deal for me. That's what made me so afraid that night, when I told you to answer the phone. I thought you were going to tell me you loved me—silly me—and I was afraid. Afraid of being hurt.' Larenz's lips tightened but he said nothing. She took a breath, spreading her hands wide. There was nothing left to hide now. 'I know it's all a bit tired and trite, but I've always had a difficult time trusting men. I didn't want them to leave the way my father always did, so I never let them get close. And when I learned about his double life, well, that sealed the deal. My heart was off-limits.'

'Sometimes,' Larenz said in a low voice, 'it's better that way.'

Ellery nodded. 'Yes, you would say that, wouldn't you? We're of the same mind, apparently.' She let out a mirthless laugh. 'That's one thing we agree on, I suppose.' She held out her hand. 'I'll take the cheque now.'

Slowly, Larenz withdrew an envelope from his breast pocket. 'What will you do with it?' he asked. 'Mow the lawns a bit more or fix the heating?' There was a glimmer of the old amusement, the old Larenz in his voice and it hurt to hear it.

'I've already arranged those,' Ellery replied flatly. 'I sold the Rolls.'

Larenz raised his eyebrows. 'You did?'

'Yes.' She crossed the kitchen and took the envelope without touching his hand. She was afraid that even that little bit of contact would weaken her resolve. She'd start to cry, or beg, or worse. She slipped the envelope into the pocket of her jumper. 'This money is actually going to charity.'

Larenz's mouth dropped open; it was, Ellery, thought, a rather satisfying sight. 'What?'

'I'm selling Maddock Manor,' she told him. 'It's time.'

'But it's your home—'

'Just like that empty palazzo is yours?' Ellery shook her head. 'I don't think so.' She paused, her gaze resting on him, taking him in and memorizing every curve and line of his face and body because she knew she would never see him again. 'They say home is where the heart is,' she said quietly, 'and it's not here.'

The words seemed to fall into the stillness, to reverberate in the silence of the room. Larenz took their double meaning for he nodded once, in acceptance.

'Goodbye, Ellery,' he said and he turned around and walked out of the kitchen.

Standing in the emptiness of the room, it occurred to Ellery that they'd both had a turn at leaving each other.

And that they were both still, and always, alone.

# CHAPTER THIRTEEN

IT WAS snowing when Ellery left the school. It didn't look as if it would stick, but the thick white flakes glittered under the London street lights as she walked down the road, busy with people leaving work, their heads lowered against the falling snow.

She'd been lucky to find a job so quickly; a literature teacher had been taking maternity leave, and the school had been glad to have a qualified teacher willing to work for just a few months. Ellery didn't mind the temporary nature of the position; she needed time to decide just what her next step would be.

Even after a month in the city, she wasn't used to the noise of the traffic, the crowds on the streets. She enjoyed going out with friends again and her regular lunches with Lil, yet she missed the one thing she thought she'd wouldn't: the peaceful solitude of her life at Maddock Manor.

She paused in front of a newsagent's; the shopkeeper was busy hauling papers and magazines back into the tiny shop, out of the wet. One glossy cover caught her eye, the splash of colour against gloomy grey all too familiar.

She reached for it, a heavy fashion magazine she'd never bothered with before.

*De Luca's Delicious Designs*, the cover read. On it, a model lounged against the fireplace, resplendent in fuchsia.

'You going to pay for that, miss?' the shopkeeper asked, a hint of surly impatience in his voice.

Ellery hesitated, and then she smiled and put it back. 'No,' she said, 'no, I'm not. Thanks, anyway.'

And she moved on.

The snow was coming down more heavily now, the grass clumped with white. Perhaps it would be a white Christmas after all; it was just a few days away. Ellery was spending the day with friends and then going down to Cornwall for Boxing Day. Afterwards, she would head back to Suffolk, to see how the renovation was going. She was looking forward to that—to seeing Maddock Manor put to good use.

In front of the block of slightly shabby mansion flats where she'd found a short-term let, she fumbled for her key. The light in front of the doorway had gone out a few weeks ago and no one had bothered to replace it, so the entryway was cloaked in darkness.

And from that darkness a voice drifted out, an achingly familiar voice that had Ellery stilling even as her heart rate kicked up a notch and her hands, still fumbling for her key, began to tremble.

'Nice shoes.'

Her fingers closed around the key as she glanced down at her wellies. She'd exchanged her school flats for the sensible boots when she'd headed out into the snow.

She lifted her head, trying to peer into the darkness. Could it really be—? 'They're just boots,' she said.

'I think I first fell in love with you when you were wearing wellies,' Larenz said, and stepped out of the darkness.

He looked so wonderfully the same, the same curly hair and glinting eyes, and yet something was different. There was a sorrow to him now, Ellery thought, a sadness in the shadow of his eyes, in the slight slump of his shoulders.

Then his words registered and her heart bumped harder.

*I fell in love with you.* 'You didn't,' she said, her voice no more than a whisper.

'I didn't fall in love with you?' Larenz filled in. His hands were shoved deep in the pockets of his coat and snowflakes dusted his hair. 'Well, I certainly tried to convince myself that I didn't. The last thing I ever wanted was to fall in love with anyone.'

Ellery's throat was tight, the possibility of hope making her dizzy with fear. Even now, she was afraid. 'Why are you here, Larenz?'

'I would have thought it was obvious. I came to say I'm sorry.'

Disappointment welled up inside her, a big dark cloud of sorrow. She nodded tightly. 'Fine. You've said it.'

'Oh, but I have a lot more to say than that,' Larenz told her softly. 'And I said I *came* to say I'm sorry. I haven't really said it yet.'

Ellery blinked hard and the threat of tears mercifully receded for a moment. 'Don't tease me,' she whispered, when what she really meant was, *Don't break my heart. Again.*

'Trust me, Ellery,' Larenz said, his voice low. 'I'm not teasing.'

She didn't trust herself to speak, so she just nodded. She unlocked the front door and led Larenz up the dim narrow stairwell to the second floor.

'It's not much,' she said as she opened the door and switched on the lights. 'It's a partially furnished sublet. But at least the heating works.'

'Indeed,' Larenz murmured. He looked incongruous in the flat's tiny lounge, with its hard ugly sofa and scarred coffee table. Ellery shed her coat and boots, dropping her handbag on the table. The actions covered the lack of words.

'Do you want something to drink?' she finally said. 'A tea or coffee?'

'I don't think what I have to say will take that long,' Larenz said after a moment, and Ellery's heart plummeted.

'Oh, all right then,' she said uncertainly and stood there, awkward in her stocking feet.

'Ellery, I love you.' Larenz met her gaze directly, his own open and honest and so achingly vulnerable. 'I love you so much that the last few months have been a living hell for me. I tried to fight it. God knows, I've been fighting it since I first laid eyes on you.' Ellery opened her mouth, but no words came out. Her mind spun. 'You had me sussed completely,' Larenz said with a small smile. 'I was afraid. I've been afraid for a long time.' He passed a hand over his face as he let out a rather shaky laugh. 'I've never admitted that to anyone— even myself—before.'

'Thank you for telling me,' Ellery whispered.

'I know the moment I decided I wasn't going to let anyone close,' Larenz told her. 'I was fourteen and my mother finally told me who my father was. I went to see him—at the palazzo I took you to. I walked up that long drive and knocked on the door.' He shook his head, remembering. 'It was a foolish thing to do, of course. I wasn't expecting him to embrace me. I wasn't that naive. But I thought…' He paused, swallowing. 'I thought he'd acknowledge me at least. Something. But he didn't. Not a word except "I don't know you". He said that twice. And, as I was leaving, he had his thugs come out and tell me they'd rough me up if I ever showed my face around there again.' Larenz sighed. 'You said your story was tired and trite, and I suppose mine is, too. We were both at the mercy of our unhappy families and let it cloud our judgement. It made us protect our hearts.'

He took a step towards her. 'But I don't want it to ruin my life. I don't want to live that way any more, Ellery. I think I convinced myself I was happy, keeping everyone at a distance, letting them be no more than a *just*, like you said.

But it's a half life at best and, even so, I think I could have gone on living it…if I hadn't met you.'

Ellery swallowed, her throat aching with suppressed emotion. The fear was crumbling away, leaving something sure and shining and true. Yet, even now, she wondered if she could trust it. 'What are you saying, Larenz?'

'I'm saying,' he said, his voice raw, 'that I'm sorry for treating you the way I did, for pushing you away because I was so afraid to pull you close. For acting like you were just my mistress when I already knew you were the love of my life.'

'Oh, Larenz—' Ellery stopped, her words choking. 'Forgiven,' she managed, her voice no more than a breath, and Larenz crossed the small space between them to pull her into his arms.

Ellery came into the embrace easily, her hands running up his arms to his shoulders and then to his face, relishing and revelling in the remembered feel of him.

'I have more to say,' Larenz told her. 'I love you, and I want to spend the rest of my life with you. It doesn't matter where. Milan or London or that Manor of yours—'

'I told you, I sold it,' Ellery said.

'I know, but we can buy it back. I know how much that house means to you.'

She shook her head. 'No, it didn't mean that much in the end. I was holding on to it because it felt like a validation of my life, my self, but it wasn't. It was just a house, and a rather unhappy one at that. I sold it to a charity.' She smiled, the knowledge still making her happy, even now. 'It's going to be a home for single mothers who need a safe place to stay. It felt like the right thing to do…considering.'

'It sounds like the right thing,' Larenz said and kissed her.

'I also wrote a letter,' Ellery continued quietly. 'To

Diane…and David. I don't know what kind of relationship we can have, but I felt like I needed to reach out to them.'

'That must have been a difficult thing to do.'

Ellery gave a shaky laugh. 'Yes, it was. I haven't heard back yet, though.'

'All these changes,' Larenz murmured. 'I suppose I should tell you I sold my palazzo, as well.'

'You did?'

'Yes, to a family with five children. They were running around the garden even as we signed the deal. It will be a happy place now. Happy and full.'

'That's good,' Ellery whispered. She buried her face in his neck for a moment, breathing in the wonderful scent of him, before she said, 'I suppose we'll need a new place to live, then.'

'Does that mean you're accepting my proposal?'

'Well…' Ellery felt a smile bloom across her face. 'I wasn't aware you'd actually asked.'

'Forgive me,' Larenz murmured and dropped to one knee. Ellery laughed aloud as he pulled a small velvet box from his pocket and flipped it open to reveal a gorgeous antique diamond ring. 'Ellery Dunant, Lady of Maddock, Lady of Shalott, lady of my heart, will you marry me?'

'Yes,' she whispered and then, louder, 'yes, yes, yes.'

She pulled Larenz to his feet and, as he claimed her mouth in a kiss once more, she knew *this* was the happy ending they'd both been searching for. Neither of them were alone or afraid; there was simply love.

Love, and bright shining joy.

# MILLS & BOON

## SEPTEMBER 2010 HARDBACK TITLES

## ROMANCE

| | |
|---|---|
| A Stormy Greek Marriage | Lynne Graham |
| Unworldly Secretary, Untamed Greek | Kim Lawrence |
| The Sabbides Secret Baby | Jacqueline Baird |
| The Undoing of de Luca | Kate Hewitt |
| Katrakis's Last Mistress | Caitlin Crews |
| Surrender to Her Spanish Husband | Maggie Cox |
| Passion, Purity and the Prince | Annie West |
| For Revenge or Redemption? | Elizabeth Power |
| Red Wine and Her Sexy Ex | Kate Hardy |
| Every Girl's Secret Fantasy | Robyn Grady |
| Cattle Baron Needs a Bride | Margaret Way |
| Passionate Chef, Ice Queen Boss | Jennie Adams |
| Sparks Fly with Mr Mayor | Teresa Carpenter |
| Rescued in a Wedding Dress | Cara Colter |
| Wedding Date with the Best Man | Melissa McClone |
| Maid for the Single Dad | Susan Meier |
| Alessandro and the Cheery Nanny | Amy Andrews |
| Valentino's Pregnancy Bombshell | Amy Andrews |

## HISTORICAL

| | |
|---|---|
| Reawakening Miss Calverley | Sylvia Andrew |
| The Unmasking of a Lady | Emily May |
| Captured by the Warrior | Meriel Fuller |

## MEDICAL™

| | |
|---|---|
| Dating the Millionaire Doctor | Marion Lennox |
| A Knight for Nurse Hart | Laura Iding |
| A Nurse to Tame the Playboy | Maggie Kingsley |
| Village Midwife, Blushing Bride | Gill Sanderson |

0810 Gen Std LP

## SEPTEMBER 2010 LARGE PRINT TITLES

# ROMANCE

| | |
|---|---|
| Virgin on Her Wedding Night | Lynne Graham |
| Blackwolf's Redemption | Sandra Marton |
| The Shy Bride | Lucy Monroe |
| Penniless and Purchased | Julia James |
| Beauty and the Reclusive Prince | Raye Morgan |
| Executive: Expecting Tiny Twins | Barbara Hannay |
| A Wedding at Leopard Tree Lodge | Liz Fielding |
| Three Times A Bridesmaid... | Nicola Marsh |

# HISTORICAL

| | |
|---|---|
| The Viscount's Unconventional Bride | Mary Nichols |
| Compromising Miss Milton | Michelle Styles |
| Forbidden Lady | Anne Herries |

# MEDICAL™

| | |
|---|---|
| The Doctor's Lost-and-Found Bride | Kate Hardy |
| Miracle: Marriage Reunited | Anne Fraser |
| A Mother for Matilda | Amy Andrews |
| The Boss and Nurse Albright | Lynne Marshall |
| New Surgeon at Ashvale A&E | Joanna Neil |
| Desert King, Doctor Daddy | Meredith Webber |

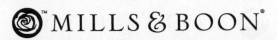

**MILLS & BOON**

# OCTOBER 2010 HARDBACK TITLES

## ROMANCE

## HISTORICAL

## MEDICAL™

0910 Gen Std LP

# MILLS & BOON

## OCTOBER 2010 LARGE PRINT TITLES

# ROMANCE

| | |
|---|---|
| Marriage: To Claim His Twins | Penny Jordan |
| The Royal Baby Revelation | Sharon Kendrick |
| Under the Spaniard's Lock and Key | Kim Lawrence |
| Sweet Surrender with the Millionaire | Helen Brooks |
| Miracle for the Girl Next Door | Rebecca Winters |
| Mother of the Bride | Caroline Anderson |
| What's A Housekeeper To Do? | Jennie Adams |
| Tipping the Waitress with Diamonds | Nina Harrington |

# HISTORICAL

| | |
|---|---|
| Practical Widow to Passionate Mistress | Louise Allen |
| Major Westhaven's Unwilling Ward | Emily Bascom |
| Her Banished Lord | Carol Townend |

# MEDICAL™

| | |
|---|---|
| The Nurse's Brooding Boss | Laura Iding |
| Emergency Doctor and Cinderella | Melanie Milburne |
| City Surgeon, Small Town Miracle | Marion Lennox |
| Bachelor Dad, Girl Next Door | Sharon Archer |
| A Baby for the Flying Doctor | Lucy Clark |
| Nurse, Nanny...Bride! | Alison Roberts |